THE BLUE GARDEN

THE BLUE GARDEN

Michael Levien

The Book Guild Ltd
Sussex, England

First published in Great Britain in 2003 by
The Book Guild Ltd
25 High Street
Lewes, East Sussex
BN7 2LU

Typesetting in Baskerville by
Keyboard Services, Luton, Bedfordshire

Printed in Great Britain by
Bookcraft (Bath) Ltd, Avon

A catalogue record for this book is available from
The British Library

ISBN 1 85776 775 6

For Myra
and in memory of S.M.L.

CONTENTS

ACKNOWLEDGEMENT

The author is grateful to Methuen Publishing Limited for permission to quote from *Conversation Piece* by Noël Coward (*Noël Coward Collected Plays: Three*), Copyright © The Estate of Noël Coward.

Every effort has been made to trace the Estate of the late Hubert Grooteclaes, whose photographic image of the Jardin du Luxembourg is reproduced on the jacket.

Fiction is the fair partner of fact.

M.L.

BEFORE

Preoccupation with thoughts of the lost person and with the events leading up to the loss is a common feature in bereaved people.

Colin Murray Parkes, *Bereavement: Studies of Grief in Adult Life*

Well, everyone can master a grief but he that has it.

Much Ado About Nothing

1

Last night I re-entered my blue garden. I go there only at night, when all is still in my rickety new world. It is not the same with daydreams, snatched reveries which swiftly become a blur and from which I awake with a start as my head snaps back from half dropping into my lap.

It is the blueness of my garden that tells me I have stolen past the silky dark veil of the late waking hours. I am in thrall to the scene: it is always the same at the start, like certain landmarks as you set out on a familiar journey. I am looking down from an upper floor of a house, of a tacitly rural aspect, on to the front drive. I cannot establish the place or the house as anywhere I have known, yet my attachment to both, my sense of belonging, is intangibly strong. There before me is a stretch of oblong-shaped lawn, and then an extended herbaceous border (its blooms are indeterminate), backed by a line of trees of a dim mauve hue, with thin aureolas of a lighter tinge, their foliage flat cut-outs. Behind is a wall, and I can see a gate there, leading into more vegetation, as yet a hidden plot neither inviting entrance nor tempting exploration along its secret paths and beside its twisting rills.

This garden, I have discovered, is a kind of shimmering screen inside my sleep. I wait for it to be lifted with the same electric sense of anticipation as if I were seated in the auditorium of a theatre before the curtain goes up. The blue garden is not the dream itself any more than a theatre curtain is an actual cornucopia, say, of the fruit

3

and flowers it displays, or whose classical emblems can clink and thrum through a haze of heavenly clouds, like the sounds of an expectant audience shifting in their seats below. I recognise it as a mere prelude, yet a vital one, a signal alerting me to events that will be played out any minute as on a brilliant floodlit stage, where an amazing new life begins when the actors stir from their waxwork postures to assume their appointed roles, in all the em-purpled classical finery, workaday costumes or shredded rags apportioned them by the playwright.

Sometimes I remain transfixed in front of this screen, as if the blue garden were all there is of 'beyond', or as if my anonymous place in the auditorium, surrounded by the hollow silhouettes of strangers, were all I should ever experience. Thus isolated, I should never travel from shadow into sunshine.

'Are you comfortable, Michael? Can I get you anything?'

I shake my head and give the nurse a vague smile. I mean to be friendly.

'Are you sure? Here, you've dropped your pen.'

The nurse, a cheery, ginger-haired auxiliary called Susan, gives me a little sidelong, knowing look, as though my recalcitrant pen has been at it again, not staying put in its allotted place on the metal-framed formica-topped adjustable little table in front of the chair where I am sit-ting, as it is supposed to do. Keep neat and tidy is the order of the day in these parts.

'Oh, sorry,' I mutter half-heartedly.

The pen must have slipped from my hand after I had scribbled the lines above, about the blue garden. I must have dozed off, yet it is only just after three o'clock in the afternoon. Nowadays I sleep sometimes out of sheer bore-dom, not because I am positively tired.

'It's nearly teatime,' Susan says, going through the motions.

Neither of us needs reminding of the hour of the day, since we both wear wrist-watches, or of mealtimes. The ritual never changes, except marginally on Sundays, when there is a short morning religious service conducted by a retired cleric for those so inclined, followed by a lunch of a traditional roast and a steamed pudding, come hail or high water, not bad for institutional food.

'I'll be bringing you a nice cup of tea.'

'Thanks.'

It is hard to believe, but I have been at Saxton House Nursing Home for nearly nine months. I came last October and it is now mid-June. A gestation period, you could say, and certainly I am feeling restive, ready mentally to pack my bags, get up and go. There is nothing to stop me really ... well, I mean I'm only sixty, which is not such a great age these days. Yes, I suppose I'm still a bit shaky on my pins after the accident, my free-fall, but I don't have to rely on a Zimmer frame. Eyesight is pretty fine. Hair, pepper and salt and still quite thick. Hands nimble enough. Legs not so wonderful, as I said, but appetite good. Mental condition? Not brilliant. I get depressed sitting here day in and day out, regurgitating the past, wondering what lies ahead. If you live too much in the past you can lose your foothold in the present, the here and now.

What I must try to do is to put my thoughts together, assemble the facts, then perhaps come to a conclusion, work out a plan, rather as I mapped out the route across France, by township, city, village, in the manner of a military strategist, before we drove South to fling ourselves in the sea, those few summers ago, Arabella and I.

2

My accident was a fatuous affair. I was alone at home one night when, answering the call of nature and failing to switch on the light, I lost my bearings momentarily and plunged down the staircase outside my bedroom. That's my recollection anyway, and it seems quite funny now, almost slapstick stuff. The fall seems to have knocked me unconscious, and I must have lain there at the foot of the stairs for – well, I don't know how long. By the time I came to it was early morning. I was in much pain, I could move only one leg, and my left arm and shoulder were in a terrible way. There was blood on my pyjamas from a cut on my forehead, it transpired, my head probably having hit the banister as I made my ungainly descent. I managed eventually to drag myself inch by inch across the floor to the telephone in the kitchen. I was put through straight away to the local hospital, who said they were sending an ambulance for me. It arrived within minutes, but first I had to crawl to the front door to unlock it and let the paramedic crew in. After the short drive to the hospital I was given a pain-killer and then it seems I passed out again soon after I tried to explain as best I could what had happened.

When I became conscious I was X-rayed and given various tests – blood pressure, cardiograph and so on. I had broken my leg in two places and my shoulder was dis-located, with my left arm badly bruised. The cut on my forehead had needed stitches, and there was a feather-light bandage over it. My head still throbbed. There was concern about giving me a general anaesthetic for the surgery that was about to take place, since the opinion had been mooted that perhaps I had not simply missed my footing but may have had a slight stroke – in a nutshell, a blackout in the night-time black-out. I couldn't quite accept this, for I had always imagined my heart to be strong, but there can never be absolute infallibility in an assessment of one's physical condition. However, after some humming and hawing and further tests, it was decided to administer a general anaesthetic before what was predictably to be a quite long-drawn-out operation.

Just before they put the mask over my face I summoned a clip from a dream I had had when under anaesthetic for a major operation as a boy. The image I plucked back from all those years past, some five decades or more, was of a red double-decker bus careering down a steep road gripped by lofty trees in green countryside; a wild image, the splash of metropolitan red incongruous amid the paintbox green of that resurrected landscape. For seconds I half hoped I might catch the same omnibus again and ride away on it, travel deep into that bosky terrain of my threatened boyhood, from which I was to awaken in the scented caress of my mother, my father towering over me like a great elm, piercing my pale little face with anxious brown eyes. Years later Arabella and I bought a large contemporary oil painting of an English country scene, complete with grazing sheep, on a summer's day. Tucked into the very top of the canvas, making its way down a distant hill, depicted in small scale but vivid detail, was a red double-decker bus, as though the artist, through some trick of the collective unconscious, had entered and shared my dream.

* * *

Saxton House, a stone building of late Georgian origin, was once the village rectory, since when it probably changed hands several times before Mr and Mrs Durrance took it over some ten years ago and converted it for its present purposes. One seldom sees dumpy, grumpy Mr Durrance, whose passion is for vintage cars, rather than old crocks of flesh and blood, but Mrs Durrance actively runs the place – from up front, as they say. She has a nursing background, I understand, and a sisterly if bossy manner, manipulating us residents rather like wayward children. She is a largish woman in her late forties with an ample bosom, thick legs and thighs and grey-yellow hair, or grey hair with highlights. She likes to be called Rosie, a name that matches her complexion but which to me always suggests a traditional young country dairymaid as fresh as cow's milk, with blonde curls and dimpled hands. Rosie Durrance is no dairymaid.

The use of Christian names or forenames for virtual strangers by the nursing staff grated on me a bit to start with, but I can more or less accept it now with equanimity. It's the great leveller, essentially a back-to-the nursery ploy that helps those concerned with our welfare to approach us old puffers and buffers with nudging familiarity, and we fall in line by dispensing with surnames among ourselves.

There are usually between eight to ten patients or inmates. Some share a bedroom, but luckily I am among those with one of my own. It is a reasonable size on the first floor and overlooks the back garden, beyond which is open countryside, fields and so on. I have some books of my own, plus a few personal items, photographs and suchlike, to remind me that I have known better days. The set of Victorian flower prints in Hogarth frames on the walls, the sort you find up and down the land in dainty tea-rooms and ribbony terraced houses, belongs to Rosie and Mr D. For furniture, as well as a couple of padded chairs, on one of which I am sitting, I have a side-table, a writing-table with a single drawer plus an upright chair, as well as the adjustable table I mentioned before. There is a built-in cupboard for my few clothes, a wash-basin and a commode for emergencies. Facing my room across the corridor is a bathroom with WC, the bath with a device for lowering and lifting the infirm or immobile, of whom I was one when I arrived here.

They somehow botched the setting of my fractured leg first time round and consequently had to rebreak it and then reset it. I think it may have become infected too. In the second operation they inserted a steel shaft down the front of my shin, which I gather will eventually have to be removed. For a while the pain was even more acute than after my original surgery, I half feared gangrene had set in, and once again I had to use crutches to get about. Now at last I can hobble around with the aid of a metal stick with a rubber ferrule, with which I could happily strike anyone who dares address me as 'Squire', though I may look the part. In fact I am obliged to exercise daily on a regular basis as much as I can.

There are two sitting-rooms on the ground floor, both ostensibly unisex. However, the large room at the front of the house, with armchairs and colour television in one half and a dining area plus piano in the other, is used mostly by the women residents and their guests, while the men tend to occupy, by convention not command, a smaller room at the back. A stale, pungent tobacco smell pervades the latter, which is never ventilated sufficiently. But it does have the advantage of french windows leading directly into the garden, where there are a couple of wooden benches, on one of which I sit sunning myself in fine weather as if I am on holiday.

At the moment there are only three other men residents,

so that apart from (Colonel) Bill Budgett, a retired regular army officer and inveterate pipe smoker, and Tim Follaton, a one-time farmer, I often have the garden to myself. When the other male resident, the snuff-taking Caspar Ayres-Southey, toddles downstairs, he remains glued to his wife's side in the front room. A slight, frail but commanding person, she lets it be known with a nonchalant air of disdain and equine flaring of her nostrils that she is of the *ancien régime*, and is prone to announce of an afternoon when the nursing staff are temporarily absent, 'The servants are having their tea.' The younger daughter of an earl, with a courtesy title, she is in fact pliant, even childlike, with her favourites among the nurses.

There is of course this attempt at democratisation at Saxton House by way of the use of forenames. This helps the nurses, as I said, in their handling of the residents. Yet the class structure among and between the residents themselves remains unobtrusively but firmly intact, despite the sharing of plight and space, crash barriers ever at the ready.

A light breakfast, as well as supper, is brought to us in our rooms, while the venue for the serving of afternoon tea and biscuits is optional, but those fit enough sit together at table for lunch (luncheon for Lady Sybil Ayres-Southey), the main meal of the day. It is hardly a convivial gathering, and seldom does anyone bother to listen to what another has to say, except on the level of enquiries about aches and pains and expectation of visitors. The main struggle of life is over for most of us; now we are left struggling for what remains of it, keeping our souls and bodies in place as best we can for the ultimate journey.

*   *   *

O for my blue garden! How I wish I could will it into my sleep, catch it with stealth by the tail. Yet it comes ... it comes. As I said at the beginning, it comes always at night, never when I slumber during the day. I have no forewarning of its imminence, it arrives when I am looking the other way, like an unexpected gift of the gods. The blue part of this garden is, as I said, a preamble, yet often – more often than not, it seems – I cannot reach past it but stay trapped inside like a restless ghost with an unfulfilled mission to smother a misdeed, to redeem some long since cancell'd woe.

Suddenly I have broken free through the garden gate, away, away. I am in Paris, dodging the bollards like upturned cannons along the pavement of the Rue Jacob. I do so with difficulty as I am carrying a heavy suitcase. I am shouting at Arabella, complaining bitterly about the mix-up over our booking at the Hôtel des Marronniers. Why didn't she confirm the booking as I asked? According to the girl at the reception desk we have arrived a day early. She regretted she couldn't offer us another room. '*Quelle horreur. Quelle horreur,*' she kept saying unconvincingly in a flat tone. '*Je suis désolée.*' She is a very pretty girl in her late twenties, her full pouting lips like wet poppies, but with an undeniably superior, down-the-nose manner, no doubt reserved for foreigners, especially *les Anglais*.

'She was no more desolated than I'm desolated,' I bellow at Arabella like a crazed bull, at which point we both have to put down our suitcases and almost cry with laughter. Heads of passers-by turn to look at the odd couple. It is acceptable to be *les Anglais excentriques* in Paris. We are heading for another hotel a quarter of a mile away, an arrangement made by the girl at the Marronniers. It's not worth the bother of going round in circles, negotiating the one-way system in a taxi to get there, though it could be the other side of the moon, burdened as we are with our luggage.

When at last we reach the alternative hotel, we ask first to see the room being offered us. Up three flights. It's not good enough, too noisy, the colours are all wrong and the atmosphere is permeated by burnt nicotine. So, down three flights. We went through this performance on numerous occasions at numerous hotels, and here we are doing the same thing all over again. We see several more rooms before reverting to the first one which, despite its being perched directly above a busy street and its noxious smell and colours, is the best available. It has only a very small chest of drawers and no hanging cupboard, but we shan't be unpacking just for one night and the double bed is so-so. We like making love especially on our first night in Paris; it is always like a honeymoon.

We are not much surprised that this hotel, with its ill-aired, grotty-looking bedrooms, still has vacancies when the rest of Paris is booked to the hilt. It is October and there is an influx of visitors to see the *prêt-à-porter* collections. There is also an Impressionist exhibition at the Grand Palais, which lies on our customary round of galleries, circling through the Jardin des Tuileries from the Louvre, Jeu de Paume and Orangerie to the Musée d'Orsay. Our trips to Paris offer always a visual feast of pictures, to which the culinary delights serve as a *sauce céleste*.

Later we go to one of our favourite haunts for dinner, it isn't quite clear now in my dream which one, and then make love on the stiff mattress of our creaky bed, laughingly wondering if the floor will collapse under our shining, locked limbs, amid our dithyrambic cries.

3

I could almost sense the after-taste of garlic in my mouth when I reawakened in the prosaic *ambience* of Saxton House, with its pong of air-freshener, old bodies and wafts of food brewing or stewing in the kitchen. I looked at the gold half-hunter I kept at my bedside, another relic from the past. It was barely 6 a.m., as yet a little too early for the daily wheels to start grinding. So I lay for a while basking in the recaptured glow of Paris by night; for moments the memory seemed almost as bewitching as the reality. The reality of my voyage beyond the blue garden or the earlier reality, I couldn't be certain which.

I got out of bed and, having put on my dressing-gown, went to the window. I looked down at the little back garden. Sparrows and a lone blackbird were busy among the bushes, whose leaves gleamed in the lemony sunlight. Later perhaps I would sit out there and read the morning paper: an old man with a stick and his memories.

Yet, in spite of my incapacity, my lameness, in my best moments I don't feel at all the dodderer I may appear to be. My hopes, in the up-circle of my cyclothymia, are still high, that in a matter of months – weeks maybe – I shall be perfectly capable of walking out of Saxton House unaided and never look back. My destiny, where I can go, seems a small problem at such times. I sold my house a while ago to finance my prolonged stint at the nursing home, it had anyway become too much of an effort living there by myself, and auctioned off most of what was left

13

of my household goods and furniture after passing on some old family pieces to Pip, my son. So I have no roof I can call my own. I half fancy going back to Paris, finding a little studio or furnished room in one of the cheaper parts of the Left Bank. Alternatively there is the South, the promise of its siren ever beckoning. Nice, perhaps, the old town, or likewise in Antibes. My needs will be simple enough. Again, I could rent a one-room apartment from which I could wander about, as of old with Arabella, watch the world pass by with a cognac in front of me at a pleasant little café, my panama at a rakish angle suggesting my nationality, as necessary, to the cosmopolitan clientele. I could scrape the occasional conversation with a congenial compatriot, keeping my eyes skinned all the while for a desirable bird of passage, a stray peahen for a roosting peacock, his tail-feathers somewhat etiolated.

It was sad disposing of so many of the personal belongings Arabella and I had accumulated over the years, with all their associations. But I feel freer without them, a touch of elation even, no longer chained to anything, to anyone. After Arabella died I put most of the silver and knick-knacks away; they had become superfluous to my life; the pleasure they once gave had been an extension of our selves, they filled an intricate, ordered pattern like planets in a solar system. Yet sometimes I mourn parting with certain paintings whose shapes and colours Arabella's eyes traced so often.

I had washed and dressed by the time breakfast was brought to me in my room – coffee and thin triangles of brown, crustless toast, with a choice of marmalade or apricot jam.

'We're early today, Michael,' says the duty nurse brightly, a wholesome girl called Alice.

'Yes we are, aren't we,' I reply in mock-nursery lingo. 'And how are we this morning, Alice?'

'Fine, fine,' Alice replies, plumping up my pillows. 'Enjoy your breakfast.'

I do enjoy the simplicity of breakfast, the pleasant sense of expectation for the day stretching ahead it brings. It was like that in Paris, Arabella and I planning our day over *grands cafés* and *croissants*, which brought to all our subsequent little outings a delightfully intimate spontaneity. At Saxton House, of course, as the day gets under way, I begin to drift somewhat, like a man stuck in a raft in an uncharted ocean encircled by a blank horizon. The activity around one, such as it is, can soon dull the spirit and merely increase one's sense of isolation. There is nowhere to *go*. I have tried venturing into the village shop, a musty-smelling little establishment with a grumpy proprietor who tends to follow one's every movement with his pebbly eyes as if watching over a prowling thief. Some of the trim front gardens of the little stone terraced houses on one side of the road running through the village are prettily laid out with their roses and seasonal flowers. I try to trap the scents, hoping one or other will transport me into another region of my life when I was younger and everything was possible.

Lunch, despite the scrappy attempts at conversation and general inattentiveness among those participating, can be amusing in a way. Bill Budgett, Tim Follaton and I are regulars, as usually are the Ayres-Southeys. Then there is a nice little Welsh lady, Megan Rees, a widow aged eighty-four, who from time to time joins us to pick at her food, concealing the remains under her knife and fork and spoon like a child; a quite charming American woman called Trudi Harrigan, also in her eighties, originally hailing from Richmond, Virginia, once a popular novelist but no longer read, I imagine, and married three times; and

15

a lame, fretful-looking German woman, another widow, by the name of Ingrid Mackintosh. The latter married a Scotsman in the Forestry Commission, whom she met shortly after the war and who brought her back to England, which she seems never to have quite adapted to or come to like. She is I gather still in her seventies, but her lameness makes her seem older, and she appears infrequently at the lunch-table.

'Have you had a good morning, Bill?' I ask of the colonel at one of these gatherings. I feel drawn to him, chaps in the same foxhole kind of thing.

'Not too bad, not too bad, thanks. Mustn't grumble.'

'These potatoes aren't cooked enough,' mutters Sybil Ayres-Southey, testily, loftily.

'Try a little butter with them, dear,' responds Megan Rees.

'Oh dear me no!' retorts Sybil, rather loudly and with a shudder, somehow raising a social drawbridge between her and the rest of the assembled company.

'They're usually *over*cooked in the traditional British way,' says Trudi Harrigan. 'You know,' she muses, 'it's sweet potatoes I miss a lot. We always had them in the South – with soured cream. Yum.'

'Sauerkraut?' asks Ingrid Mackintosh in a rare intervention.

'No, ma'am, *soured cream*,' Trudi repeats, holding herself back, no doubt.

All this about potatoes.

A faint groan rumbles from beside Sybil Ayres-Southey. It comes from her husband Caspar, himself plain Mr. No, he is not in any discomfort, he just wants the salt and pepper, which are out of his reach. Sybil doesn't pass him anything except an occasional look of exasperation. 'Did you see *Mr* Durrance this morning?' she asks of no one in particular.

'Yes, yes I did, Lady Sybil,' says Tim Follaton eagerly, no doubt anxious to placate her ladyship, whom he invariably addresses by her handle.

'*Dreadful* little man,' says Sybil. 'Thankful we must all be that *Mrs* keeps him well out of sight. Anyway, he didn't venture into the house, just snooped about among the cars in the forecourt like some miserable traffic warden.'

'Whatever does he do with himself all day, I wonder?' enquires Trudi mischievously, ever the novelist hatching plots. This will surely test the others.

'Does it matter, as long as he stays out of sight?' retorts Sybil.

'I wonder what's for pudding?' asks Megan Rees keenly after a pause. She has evidently picked enough at her main course, unfinished bits of meat and vegetables discarded in their customary position under her knife and fork.

'Treacle tart and custard, I believe, Megan. I asked Alice this morning,' says Trudi.

There is now an extended interlude in the chit-chat during which the others continue masticating their food, the silence punctuated by the click of cutlery against plates, the clack of dentures, the bat-squeak of a hearing aid.

'I suppose that fella Durrance does the gardening next door and makes himself generally useful around the house,' mumbles Bill Budgett, as if returned at last from an extended recce over the garden wall, where the Durrances have their own private quarters, a converted coach-house. A mission not quite worthy of a mention in despatches, and Bill's tardy observation is ignored by the others.

And that was pretty well the end of the lunchtime conviviality for that day, fairly typical, bar the grunts and grimaces and vague enquiries about the others' health among the nibblers, of so many that followed.

It intrigues me that the members of our little group,

each and every one of them, were once young, full of passion and promise, not so much sizing up the difficulties ahead, but rather prepared to step into the unknown, make stabs in the dark, uninhibited by foreknowledge. It fascinates me, for instance, that handsome Tim Follaton, with his cracked and weathered features and West Country burr, a hardy-looking survivor, when years and years ago he was jilted by his one and only girl-friend, never looked at anyone else and consequently has remained a firm bachelor. Bill Budgett, one gathers, was a run-of-the-mill member of a county regiment, though with some service in the Far East, never quite defined. Innuendo has filtered through the ranks in the nursing home that the Japs removed his testicles, which may have influenced his former wife to run off with a brother officer, fully equipped in that area – 'all balls and brass', as Bill was heard to mutter of the brazen usurper one evening in the men's room after a sundowner too many. Though he plays the type-cast colonel with some of his more monosyllabic utterances, somehow the most military aspect of Bill, a shambling barrel of a man of average height with a round, oak-apple face and bald pate, is his briar pipe, the white-stained stem of which, when he gestures with it on occasion to emphasise a point, resembles a pistol or revolver. You have to dig hard to extract anything from him of his army days and he never mentions the war, no doubt because of its poignant outcome for him.

Megan Rees, on the other hand, was ever a happy soul, with a dear husband and two dear children, who have brought her several equally dear grandchildren. A neat, white-haired little woman with pallid, peachlike skin and a delightful soft Welsh accent, she has no complaints about Saxton House, its staff or its inmates. She quite revels in being 'waited on hand and foot', as she puts it. She has never known the luxury of such personal attention before, having always been the willing drudge, cooking and cleaning and caring for her husband and offspring until separated by death, as with her husband, or they left the family nest, near Bangor, to make their own way in the world, as was the case with her children when they grew up. Megan shares a room upstairs with another woman resident called Miss Ashtead, or Doris, bedridden and speechless since she suffered a stroke more than a year ago. For this reason I have never met her, though Megan speaks of her from time to time as an ever-live presence, having found ways of communicating with her despite her companion's disability. This doesn't surprise me of Megan, whose gentle sweetness and patience shine out for all to see, prone as she may be through mental lapses or deafness to grab the wrong end of the stick at our lunchtime gatherings.

I shall return to some of the others later, though in each case, as with those introduced above, one can do little more than lightly sketch in their particularities, gleaned over months from random morsels. You can never quite see the young in the old, the pink, elastic flesh that wens and wrinkles have corrupted, the once bright eyes behind those yellowing marbles with their fractured capillaries. One must be elderly oneself to understand properly how many worlds away is the present from the past, yet memories of one's young, supple figure can play curious tricks, occasionally teasing one's grounded limbs like a man crazed on hallucinogens who suddenly leaps from an upper window in broad daylight, imagining he can fly.

4

I can fly in my dreams. At first I sometimes detect a
luminescent band around the outer perimeter of the blue
garden, like trembling gold wire. It is a thin frame
achieved by light shining behind the blueness, so that
when I feel I may become stranded like some lost spirit,
I draw comfort from this reminder of my previous som-
nambulant excursions, that all is still possible if one can
simply wait and watch without fretting. Soon enough –
tonight, tomorrow – I shall escape my blue chrysalis like
a metamorphosed butterfly and assume once again the
miracle of flight.

Flight. Escape. I have always thought of running away –
eloping, hiding, freeing myself, vanishing. Escaping from
school, quitting a job, making off with another man's wife,
living incognito, by stealth, leaving the world guessing as
to my whereabouts. The world? Well, those in my small
world.

I ran away from home once as a boy after a row with
my father. I stayed out for several hours, it was winter, and
while the search for me was still going on, when it grew
dark and flashes of torchlight were at a distance and the
excited barks of our dogs grew faint, I crept back and hid,
crouching uncomfortably, in a bush just outside our house.
This will teach him, I thought.

My father's distressed anger when eventually I emerged,

20

cold and stiff from my hiding-place, was quickly dispelled by joy at my rediscovery. Dad wanted to make things right with me, it was clear. 'Where on earth did you get to, Mikey?' he asked gently.

I couldn't admit where I ran to ground, it would have sounded too tame. 'Oh, miles away,' I replied mysteriously.

'You are a funny boy,' he said, ruffling my hair, his deep laugh making me forgive him in my heart.

Half the fun of running off is to keep people guessing, I suppose, just as I did my father. Yet there is the business, too, of being unable to bear too much reality when the thrill of the chase temporarily recedes. I fear boredom as others fear loneliness. I can accept being lonely as a part of the human condition, like hunger and thirst, but not as a prisoner.

After I had taken early retirement, Arabella and I began travelling regularly abroad, to Spain, Italy and North Africa, but mostly to France. Each time it was as if we were making a dash to freedom. We were happy enough in our day-to-day lives yet we relished going 'on holiday'. Probably my restlessness affected her: she might start by making objections ('But we have just *been* away'), but soon enough she succumbed and then became as enthusiastic as I for yet another excursion. Maps and guide-books would come tumbling out, timetables, resorts, routes, hotels would be considered. Then I would sketch out an itinerary, detailing more and more as I went along, dates, distances, places of historical or architectural interest, places where perhaps we would avoid other English tourists. (Why English? Germans and Japanese with their cameras were everywhere. I recall groups of Japanese like nibbling maggots coiled for culture around the glass pyramid by the Louvre.) Suddenly *Michelin*, with all its hieroglyphic symbols, became pulsatingly alive. We fantasised about staying at hotels listed with five turrets and five forks, signifying *grand luxe et tradition*, even those with four turrets and four forks (*grand confort*), and then were contented enough realistically to consider humbler, two-turreted ones with two forks (*de bon confort*), and those with a single roof and fork (*assez confortable*). Finally, or rather penultimately, came the hotels or hostelries symbolised by a wide inverted V – that is to say, a sloping roof – over a wineglass and fork (*simple mais convenable*). The latter could sometimes be *charmants*, especially so after a long, tiring drive, with an atmosphere redolent of the France we were seeking and less likely to be found in the more pretentious hotels with their opulent appointments and obsequious or patronising staff.

The act of opening *Michelin* was already to begin another journey: a square of pale green became a lush *bois* or *jardin des plantes*; you could see the traffic careering along the double-red lines of motorways; alps rose from flat contours; a church, depicted by a symbol like a silver hallmark, popped up from the page into relief, changing perspective as one looked up at it in the mind's eye like the shifting twin steeples of Martinville viewed by the young Marcel from Dr Percepied's speeding carriage before it clattered on towards Combray. Even as I jot down these random images I sense the urge to take off again, but I resist reaching out for my *Michelin*, uncertain if the stirring of happy memories as I rustle the pages will revive anew the pain of my final severance from Arabella, as compellingly as I might hear again our feet shifting through the amber leaves at Malmaison where we picknicked among the poor, sad Empress Josephine's dead dreams.

'Teatime already?'

I look up, startled, as Alice appears by my side. I have quite lost track of the time.

'No, no. You must have been dreaming, Michael. It's not even lunchtime yet,' Nurse Alice says brightly. 'It's the sun, probably. It's really very warm in here this morning. It's a beautiful day.... Here, you've dropped your pen.'

'Ah.'

Alice puts my ever-wayward pen back on my adjustable table. I can tell that, not for the first time, she is quite intrigued by the wire-bound notebook in which I am trying to make sense of my life as well as help while away the hours in what otherwise might be long, blank days. She is right, it is getting hot in my room, airless, and I ask her to open the window wider.

Alice does so and flits around, her eyes darting hither and thither. She is short and, as I said earlier, wholesome, with mouse-coloured hair, a snub nose, cute little dimples and a charming hint of a moustache above her delicate pink lips. I admire her nice, firm, smooth young legs and arms, but as if she were my daughter, not as a lecher. She is sweet and caring, with an easy manner and crisply efficient.

'Now, you're not going to nod off again, are you?' she says. 'You don't want to miss a nice lunch.'

'No, I'm all right, thanks.... Thanks so much, Alice. I'm looking forward to some stimulating chat.'

Alice chuckles, putting her forefinger to her lips as she leaves the room, in a mock-conspiratorial gesture. I could have kissed her just for that. She makes me feel a proper person, apart from the rest; she senses my intricacies.

I don't know if this could be said of Rosie Durrance, who now bursts into my room in a flurry. She looks flushed and agitated. Her straits must be dire.

'The lift has broken down,' she announces, thrusting her head forward like a strutting chicken as she grunts and groans. 'Just what we need. These things always seem to happen at the weekend. God knows when the

23

maintenance people will be able to send an engineer. They were very evasive on the telephone, though I reminded them sharply that they are supposed to be under contract to effect repairs within twenty-four hours.'

'Oh dear, what a bore,' I say somewhat speciously. 'Rather puts the lid on things.'

'Indeed, yes.... Lids. I'm sorry, Michael, but you'll have to have your lunch brought up to you, unless you feel you can brave the stairs, which I *don't* somehow recommend.'

I have tried the stairs occasionally, but even with the help of a stick it's a tedious, long-drawn-out business. It is almost easier mounting the staircase than descending, which increases the possibility of losing one's balance.

'Bang goes my "community lunch",' I say in quotes.

'And bang goes community singing tomorrow with old Father Whatsit, by the looks of it.... Still, think of all the elderly people who lived here in the past. They must have managed without lifts and things.'

The thought of generations of old people trudging up and down the staircase, straining corsages and crinolines, of spatted, bewhiskered clergymen spouting snatches from the Scriptures as they went about their business, slips wilfully into my head.

'And even without you, Rosie,' I say teasingly.

Rosie gives me a winsome smile. She is easy to flatter. Sometimes, I am tempted to think, she positively flirts with me in a lubricious sort of way. Yesterday, for instance, after I had had my supper and she was on her evening rounds, she came very close to me as I sat in my room and half whispered in my ear: 'You know, we almost had to trick Bill into having a bath this morning. He's a *dirty boy*.' As she leaned towards me to proffer this crumb of tittle-tattle she exposed rather more than a fair share of her bobbing breasts, inviting me I fancied to touch one or plunge my hand into her cleavage as if to retrieve a detached bead or errant lump of sugar. I affected not to notice, considering it was up to Mr D alone to trawl the mellifluous if not quite secret recesses of her body.

'It must be difficult handling old chaps like us,' I mumbled defensively, though immediately I wished I hadn't said 'handling', which sounded vaguely provocative.

'Old? No, not you, Michael. You pitch in.... Well, you're part of the furniture – I mean that as a compliment. And I know you've been through hell with your poor leg. You're considerate with the nurses, though of course you're *reserved*.' She flashed me a smile, as if to comment on my straight-bat response to her flighty lunge. 'If only some of the others would follow your good example.'

This morning Rosie hasn't time to linger. 'I must go now,' she says, matter-of-factly. 'We'll keep you in the picture, of course, about the lift.'

She leaves a faintly fruity aroma behind her – grapes, cassis...? I shan't allow it to disturb my dreams.

5

More than a week goes by before the maintenance people fix the lift. There is some part that has to be sent from the Midlands. The usual thing. One could have flown a hundred times back and forth to South America or somewhere in the time it takes to deliver the vital part to Saxton House.

Never mind; such crises inspire initiative. After a couple of days I have grown restless confined to my room and am determined to leave it. It is perfect summer weather, a bright sun with a cooling breeze, not too hot at present for July. Having heaved myself down the staircase, I soon tire of reading the newspaper in our back garden, watching Bill Budgett stoking and puffing at his smouldering volcano of a pipe, and start to venture forth into the village. In fact Bill asks if he may accompany me and I can hardly say no. He seems such a harmless old wreck, my foxhole sharer, and besides I am always minded to think of his testicles, or lack of them (on that account alone, perhaps he feels shy of being helped in the bath), and the heartache he must have endured on the breakup of his marriage. It gives me a twinge of unease, as if I have an unfair advantage over him, though we aren't exactly competing for anyone or anything.

Bill must have read my thoughts, for no sooner have we emerged from the fusty-musty village shop, where he purchased some more pipe tobacco, than he says, after relighting his briar for the umpteenth time: 'Bloody man went off with my wife just after the war. I suppose you know – these things get around.'

I nod.

'Fella in my regiment, so-called "brother officer". Brother, huh!' He splutters over his pipe, then wipes the spittle from his lips with the back of his hand. 'Young subaltern, junior to me too. Pipsqueak, but must have rutted like a stag.' For a moment he savours his description, though it is less than newly minted, with a twitch – or is it a twinkle? – in his small brown eyes. 'You see,' he continues, lowering his voice as we coast near the church graveyard, as if to prevent the dead from overhearing his terrible secret, 'when the Japs castrated me ... they sliced my pills off, you know, bloody butchers ... after the war when I was reunited with Vera, I couldn't ejaculate any more. I couldn't *roger* properly....' His voice trails away, as if these jerky revelations have winded him.

I hate it when men talk to me about their sex lives: their schoolboy lewdness, their vaunted conquests, their suspect prowess. But Bill looks so melancholic as we halt all of a sudden outside the graveyard, he touches a deep chord of sympathy in me. There is nothing I can say, of course, that is worth saying; almost any comment would be inappropriate in the circumstances.

'Vera, you see ... well, you know what women are.... Vera liked being bedded. Riding and rogering – that's what she went for, huh, that's what tickled her fancy. Well, she had a horse all right, bloody great chestnut called Brute – funny name, not at all, fitted him to a T – but I was no use to her any more after Hirohito's lads had done with me....'

'I'm sorry, Bill,' I say after a long pause. I felt I must say something, anything, to pierce the bubble of pain floating in the radiant air. The breeze now stifled, all is still.

27

Bill looks like a stricken beast. He seems about to keel over in agony, but he merely bends to expel the ashes from his pipe by tapping it against the heel of his shoe. Then he stands up again and lets out a deep sigh but says nothing.

I am still thinking about Bill's private confession to me when I return from our stroll and I have climbed half-way up the stairs to return to my room. I am feeling a bit weary from the effort and pause for a moment, leaning on the banister.

The next thing I know I am splayed out on my back at the bottom of the staircase, my legs half on the last few steps, a searing pain in the small of my back. It is as if time has stood still and I am at home all those months ago when I made my first fateful plunge.

Susan and Alice, assisted by Ben, a male nurse, loosen my collar and then support my head and shoulders as very carefully they move me on to a stretcher. My mind is confused. I don't know quite how or why I fell this time. My legs seemed to crumble under me ... I recall feeling dizzy. Did I faint?

Now Rosie Durrance is standing over me. I can see up her loose summer dress to her panties. She must be off duty. Those big thighs, a great bulge at her crotch, a veritable mound of Venus. She is always exposing parts of her body to me, but I am less than ever capable – *in a position*, ha ha – of taking advantage of her teasing ministrations. That this is no time for flirtation she makes plain when she announces commandingly: 'The ambulance is on its way.' Then, bending down and in a softer tone, she asks: 'Are you in a lot of pain? Are you quite comfortable?' A luscious odour of fruit seeps from her bosom to my head.

'Yes I'm OK, thank you. My back's hurting a bit.' A stiff upper lip now with Rosie and she may feel moved to reward her fallen hero with a private view of her Venusian delights when I am back to full strength. Such Great Insights flash to mind in unexpected moments. Yet how can I want to take her now in my befuddled, crippled state?

I must have lost consciousness then, for the next thing I knew I was back in the hospital. Evidently I was screened off in a ward, and periodically a nurse, then in turn a consultant and the orthopaedic surgeon came to inspect me, feel my pulse, take my temperature, check my blood pressure. My plated leg – both my legs – are it seems un-affected by my fall, thank God. It is my back where the trouble lies. X-rays revealed that I have a condition called *spondylolisthesis*, in short a slipping forward of the base of my spine. It is a congenital condition, weakened by physi-cal strains and stresses in childhood and adolescence, and I must have wrenched my back as I tried vainly to cling on to the banisters on my downward stumble. There is no 'cure' for my condition, but remedial exercises can be effective, I am told. With the help of a corset, for which I have already been measured, I should gradually be able to achieve the same so-called mobility I enjoyed previously. Meanwhile I must rest flat on my back.

The dizzy spell I complained of remains a mystery – shades of my original fall. Yet they can find nothing wrong with my heart, my blood pressure is excellent, good for a man half my age. Anyone can faint – and perhaps the sun had been too much for me? It had of course been a hot afternoon, particularly when the wind dropped, the day I went on my emotive outing with Bill Budgett.

Pip came to see me in the hospital. He flew from New York, said he was due to come over anyway and had simply put forward his schedule. He is in the wine business – import and export – and appears to enjoy his new job and the stimulus of life in America, where he has now been living for several months. He sat for a long time by my bedside. He looked thoughtful but seemed quite relaxed. In fact he stayed overnight in a spare bed in my ward, which was nice of those concerned and for me. He said he had been praying for me. I noticed tears in his eyes as he told me this, and I felt touched. We hadn't seen each other since he left London, but I am thankful that the essential bond between us is intact. We have had our differences, but that is all water under the bridge. He has a good wife and two lovely small children, a boy and a girl. He told me a third child is on the way. 'So we have a dynasty in the making,' he said.

I remained in the hospital for a further ten days, under 'general observation' and until the promised corset was ready for me. The day after Pip's visit Rosie drove over from the nursing home. I thought how compassionate she is, belying her habitual bossyboots manner.

'My dear boy,' she said kindly. 'This is becoming a habit.'

'I know.'

She took my hand in hers and held it for a while, but not seductively, and I felt ashamed of my sudden lustful urge as I had lain on my back and she had succoured me by the staircase at Saxton House, tantalising me with her aroma of fruit. Now that fragrance hovered again by my bedside, but in a comforting way like the magic scent of my mother, for which I still search the air.

'We must keep you in one piece now,' Rosie said as she stood up to go. 'With the lift back in action you won't need to bother with the stairs any more – fingers crossed.'

6

My back is still troubling me. Rosie insists on my getting
up and walking about as much as I can. I am helped by
my corset, which acts as a support as well as restricting
my movements. For example, there is no question of my
being able to bend down suddenly to pick up something
– my wayward pen, for instance. I am gaining more assurance, physically, if not more strength, as a result; yet I feel
depressed, wondering in renewed waves of morbidity if
ever I shall leave this place, if ever I can build a life for
myself again in the outside world.

The nurses try to cheer me up, and some of the others
have rallied round – Bill and Tim and Trudi Harrigan
have each come to my room for a chat. Bill wasn't very
forthcoming – perhaps he thinks he overstepped the mark
in our village meander – and Tim, tall, heavily built,
tawny-complexioned, with curly, waxy grey hair and large,
horny hands, which he held folded in front of him as he
stood by the window, bumbled on about the continuing
arid weather and how this may affect the harvest and so
forth, an understandable concern in an ex-farmer but it
almost set me off counting sheep as a distraction.

I find Trudi a most appealing, companionable person
and she hints of a past of many layers. What immediately
strikes one about her is her whiteness. Her skin, her face
especially, is almost chalk white – even more pallid than
that of Megan Rees – and her hair, which she wears in
page-boy style, is as blanched as snow, so that sometimes,

when you catch sight of her across a dim-lit room, she seems ethereal, ghostlike. With the black shawl she invariably wears over her shoulders – of chiffon or wool, according to the season – she looks of another age and could as well be an ancestral portrait that has slipped out of its gilt frame on the wall. Not quite Whistler's mother, she's the wrong shape. Though she must once have stood above average height, she has shrivelled in old age and walks with a stoop, her head bent as though she is scouring the ground in front of her for something she has let fall from her trembly hands. She has an engaging smile and a mild Southern accent which I shan't attempt to reproduce, her voice crackling as she talks animatedly.

She tells me that her first husband was a childhood sweetheart, but they drifted apart and ultimately divorced. Her middle husband was the Canadian-born communist poet and critic Claud Schott (she pronounces it *Schart*, dragging the 'a' like a true Southerner). He must have been an unlikely candidate for Trudi's hand in marriage, or anyone else's for that matter, and I told her so. She laughed and was interested when I said that I had been acquainted with Claud as a young man at the time I had just started to work in publishing. I used to see him in one or other of the Soho haunts of the day – the Gargoyle, Mandrake, Caves de France. Invariably he was the worse for drink, and aggressive, but he rather made a point of being friendly to me. Maybe he saw me as of possible use to him as a publisher, though I don't think he was cynically motivated, denouncing the Establishment in all its guises, smooth-tongued literary hounds included, at every opportunity. This must have been before he married Trudi, by which time I had left London.

Soon enough, and sure enough, Trudi divorced drunken Claud and returned to America, where eventually she remarried, her spouse this time an affluent business man.

She took up writing fiction between husbands as a means of supporting herself. However, after publishing a score or so of novels she decided, some ten years ago when arthritis began seriously to affect her hands, that enough was enough. Besides, by then she had gone out of fashion and the once large sales of her books had dwindled considerably. She looked at my small medley of books and said, disarmingly: 'I can see you wouldn't like the sort of crap I wrote. But I was darned lucky – my yarns made me a packet and, what's more, I *enjoyed* writing them.'

Her third husband, an Anglo-American, left her well provided for, and when he died she returned to live in England, 'to watch the Old World crumble'. Now she is crumbling too, but she says she'll be happy to spend the rest of her days at the nursing home. 'I could probably afford something grander – well, you know, it's not the greatest here – but frankly I *don't* like things too tiptop, and I *do* like Rosie and the nurses,' she said. 'I'm a warts-and-all dame.'

In turn, she asked me – cautiously – about my life and I filled in some gaps, but I am reluctant to spill the beans, so to speak, while I am still juggling with them.

We talked on for a while about our fellow-inmates at the home and of our general likes and dislikes. 'That Caspar's a dark horse,' she said mysteriously, with a smile. Then, before she left the room, Trudi looked at me hard with her clear blue eyes, her small, beaklike nose giving her an owlish look, and said with evident concern: 'You must leave here, Mike, just as soon as you can. This is no place for hiding.'

7

My blue garden seems to be eluding me these days, or it may be that I am not of a mind, not yet poised, to re-enter it. *This is no place for hiding.* Trudi's admonishment (how percipient she is) circles my mind; but she knows nothing of my inner refuge, the sanctuary I find when the cobalt screen of my demi-world lifts or dissipates like fog in sunlight as I slide deeper and deeper into luminiferous sleep. It may be that a part of me dreads re-entering that recess of my subconscious where old demons lie with daggers drawn, ready to thrust them again into my side. My wounds have not healed; I fear more pain.

Yet reason tells me in the long daylight hours that I must face facts. Soon it will be October, that fateful month which was the harbinger of good and ill, whose glorious copper hues burnished the Parisian streets and sky as if spilling from certain canvases in which the earlier off-spring of their ancestral branches were magically reflected by the Impressionist masters. It was as though, standing on the bank of a still, unruffled lake, you might be tricked for a moment by the mirror-images, so that reaching for what you took to be the overhanging shoots of a tree, you find yourself plunging into water.

A smell of earth and leaves pomaded the air as I strolled with Arabella, her arm threaded through mine, in the Jardin du Luxembourg. We sat down for a while as we had so many times beside an upper terrace and idly watched the passers-by – couples sunning themselves or circling the pond, students reading, with feet propped up on spare, spindly garden chairs, their peripatetic gestures and attitudes melding into a tellurian cavalcade across the green and russet landscape.

I can remember nothing of what we said. All is scents and images, the thrum of traffic muffled by trees, from which pigeons, their clattering feathers dappled by sunlight, dived for crumbs of cake and bread dispersed by solitary old ladies seated at café tables amid the richly polished horse-chestnuts scattered on the yellowing grass. If I could catch an echo of the words we spoke, especially Arabella's, I would hold it close to my ear like a whispering seashell for a message. What might she have uttered that I could still clutch in my memory like a golden locket with her portrait, a tuft of her hair, in my hand? Might a single word, so recalled, bring back to me her essence, a single droplet of sound her voice, a hint of the oval of her mouth, the carmine lips which had entranced or maddened me? As the chime of a distant bell evokes a church, a village, a way of life out of sight across a valley, so might her presence be transported back to me from our lost domain.

But those last few hours we spent together remain silent, there is no buzz coiled in my eardrum, as of music on the cylinder of an old phonograph, that I can unroll and replay with the needle of my mind, no signal, no flashing prism to pinpoint the precise moment of decline, the moment Arabella started edging towards her impending doom.

Perhaps it is as well. A thin cry in a moment of distress can bring relief or herald disaster, the scratch of a pen unleash the dogs of war. It can be so small a thing, a single broken link, that dislodges and scatters a whole chain of events from its expected pattern. It is as well that I am not left with the vain notion that the retraction, say, of some trivial remark might have speeded up events for vital seconds, or if Arabella or I had said more of this or that in such-and-such a place, it might have delayed her headlong steps. Why should I torment myself now with futile conjecture, try to backtrack on the irreversible?

I tell myself that if I committed an error of some kind, made a remark of a sort that I immediately regretted but couldn't withdraw, it is I who have suffered as a consequence, I who as a result have had to endure her permanent loss. A fearful emptiness inhabits me as I set this down. You can call it self-pity, but I believe it is more than that, more poignant: it is a sense that all the love I gave Arabella somehow failed her in the end; all the days, hours, years of adoration I lavished on her, the rapture we shared, have condemned me, a so-called survivor, to a life of exile from reality. In place of her face, eyes, skin, body, hair, her hands, her voice, her entire lovely being, I am left reaching for the dream-world of my blue garden as recompense for what I have lost. Yet even as I attempt to diminish it, I become aware once more of its puissance, of its almost magnetic power to draw me back in and beyond its ephemeral veil where I can reconnect with Arabella, with what went before, before everything seemed inexorably to fall apart.

And so it is that I find us once again leaving the Jardin du Luxembourg, our destiny an obscure question of synchronicity or, let us say, in the lap of the gods. We haven't gone far, we have walked for only a few minutes, progressing slowly down the Rue de Tournon towards the Boulevard St Germain, when we start a quarrel. It has to be said that we do bicker a lot from one day to the next, we have always done so; it is a habit honed on the keen edges of our reflexes. After all, we are very different people: whereas I hold back, keep my cards close to my chest so to speak, Arabella is vivaciously open, and in Paris of all cities (she sees it as her spiritual home) she is positively effervescent. And then while I am contemplative, Arabella is quick-thinking, tending towards impatience when she considers I am dragging my feet unduly. Yet of the two of us I am the more impulsive, and so on.... Our disparities, to which we give expression in verbal crossfire, rather than divide us, spark off the essential *frisson* that keeps our relationship vibrant and confidently alive. We discuss books and pictures, love and death, freely and with equanimity, never mind if our tastes and opinions do not correspond. Such conversations are among our pleasures, and each time we try to grapple with our likes and dislikes in a private, unconvoluted way, naïvely even, it opens windows a chink wider into the mystery of art and imagination. From time to time Arabella emphasises that she would like to have 'a good death'. Does she mean that she wants to be prepared for it as for a thief in the night? I can't recall her reply if ever I asked the question....

More often than not, it is on a banal level that we clash, and thus it is today as we turn, without paying any attention to directions, towards the Place St Sulpice. Maybe we are arguing about where we are and where we are heading. It is the last day of our visit here, so I have reserved a table for lunch at a favourite restaurant of ours on the Quai des Grands Augustins. Therefore we do have a destination, and it seems that if we continue on our present errant course we shall arrive at the restaurant well after the appointed time. As Arabella knows full well, I am somewhat obsessive about punctuality.... Now the clock of St Sulpice is striking – is it one o'clock already?... I am in a sweat of anxiety.

*　*　*

37

I come to with a jolt, the sound of the church bell resonating in my ears. I am still sweating, and my back is aching too. Did I fall down and hurt it in the street? Where is Arabella? This can't be Paris.

Of course it isn't. Instantly I am aware that the coincidence of the chiming of the village church clock in Saxton in the heart of the English countryside with that of St Sulpice in the 6th *arrondissement* of Paris is what confused me. I feel cheated, that I have been shifted from one set piece to another as on a revolving stage without forewarning, without consultation, like a puppet on a string. A mixture of frustration and relief follows – frustration that I didn't reach the restaurant after all; relief that I have been rescued on the brink of catastrophe, literally saved by the bell; though simultaneously I am all too aware that it is only a matter of stalling, of staying the execution, the forward motion of Arabella's limbs and mine merely remaining suspended in the Place St Sulpice as if halted on a reel of film, the projector having packed up. The lights in the cinema have been switched on, I am back in the present, but sooner or later when the machinery is fixed, they will be dimmed and I shall be propelled anew through the blue haze to find myself beside Arabella, ready to resume our progress towards the inevitable as the clock of St Sulpice strikes the hour like a death-knell.

All the while I am left wondering whether the route we took when we left the Jardin du Luxembourg was purely fortuitous, as were so many steps we made in our shared lives, or under the influence of some malevolent force. The irony is that in this case, on this of all occasions, Arabella is not able to give an opinion.

8

At Saxton House life goes on much as usual. Except, of course, for the *scandal*. This involved – of all people – Caspar Ayres-Southey. He has always impressed me as a limp old duck, or rather drake, almost totally under his wife's spell, with whatever stuffing he may once have had long since knocked out of him. It is not so.

The little incident involved him and one of the nurses, Josephine by name – or Little Jo as some of us affectionately call her. A petite blonde with bright blue eyes, she is very pretty in a Barbie doll way and has a soft, soothing voice to go with it. Anyway, one morning last week she was helping Caspar in his bath and, so the story goes, soaping him between his legs when – *oop-la!* – probably much to his own astonishment Caspar suddenly achieved a spectacular if not handsome erection. Not content with this immodest miracle, he caught hold of Little Jo and somehow pulled her on top of him into the bath. Conflicting accounts have been circulating as to what happened next, and the more scatalogically embroidered ones are obviously to be taken with a pinch of salt – or snuff, as Trudi appositely says. Among the more apocryphal of these is the version that has Caspar manipulating Little Jo, or exciting her to such an extent, that he was able to mount her in the missionary position in the tub, his paunch enveloping her like a rubber girdle. Whatever occurred, when Little Jo emerged from the bathroom she was dripping wet and, as some wag mischievously put it

(Ben, the Asian male nurse, I gather), with the fishy look of a gratified mermaid in her eyes.

News of this happening spread in the home like a bush fire. While Little Jo herself appears unabashed by her Neptunian encounter, Rosie Durrance is said to have been furious with Caspar (yet another 'dirty boy' in her midst) and to have given him a stern private reprimand – the equivalent in nursing-home terms of six of the best if not forty lashes beneath the mainmast. Certainly Caspar seems chastened, his hangdog countenance these past few days being more pronounced than usual. Nevertheless when I see him at lunchtime I detect an air of triumph about his hitherto flaccid expression, almost a look of smugness. Trudi tells me with her novelist's nose for sniffing out the nitty-gritty that in his youth Caspar was something of a ladies' man, in fact a regular woman-chaser, which earned him the nickname the Salacious Shrimp, more on account of his diminutive stature and once pink-and-white complexion than because of any predilection he may have had for aquatic fun and games. Now I know of what Trudi must have been hinting when she referred to Caspar in our earlier chat as a 'dark horse', no doubt not then wishing to flourish his crustacean sobriquet, whose origin I might well have pressed her to reveal. She now dubs him the *Tiger Prawn*.

In spite of his second-fiddle role beside Sybil, who outshines him effortlessly at the lunch-table, or indeed his rascally escapade in the bathroom, Caspar is noticeable for his quiet good manners. For example, unlike his wife, he is good at passing the salt and pepper; and he says good-morning or good-afternoon with a certain *élan* or old-world charm, looking you in the eye. He does nothing with a flourish, yet you can still recognise the dandy in him, small touches of it in his apparel. He wears somewhat faded tweeds; but the creases of his trousers are like knife-edges and his cracked brown brogue shoes are always highly polished. His shirts are a trifle frayed at the collar, but the cuffs are chicly narrow, brought together just below the sleeves of his jacket with fine gold links, and into the left-hand sleeve he tucks a coloured silk handkerchief. This he uses to dab his pitted red nose discreetly after taking his snuff – though never at the lunch-table – which he keeps in an elegant silver-gilt snuffbox incised with a monogram. On the little finger of his left hand he wears a signet-ring with a pale-blue bloodstone, and alongside it a gold wedding-ring. Occasionally, perhaps as a mark of respect as much as of pride, he wears the blue and red tie of the Household Brigade, of which at the peak of his womanising days he was a member, serving in the Blues. It was while he was still a dashing young blood that Sybil, a beauty who stood out among the throng of cajoling flappers, caught hold of him, or rather netted her naughty Shrimp, and then proceeded to marry him, disregarding the restraining hands of family and friends who considered her catch had too much of a dance-band outlook on life, in other words that he was an unmitigated playboy. If subsequently Caspar sometimes wriggled back into amatory pools, Sybil resolutely turned a blind eye. Wherever he then philandered, she knew she had her darling aquanaut by the nose.

Sybil is above idle gossip, and although she must have heard about the bathtub affair, to all outward appearances, so far as she is concerned, it might never have happened. She is too well bred to share any thoughts she may have on the matter with anyone else, save possibly one of her pet nurses, and she treats Caspar as peremptorily as ever. At lunchtime I watch her hands, mentally comparing them with those depicted in Sargent's famous painting of a seraphic young Lady Sybil in the National Portrait Gallery, the once long, slim fingers now gnarled, their

41

freckles melding with old-age spots. And then I think, not for the first time, what a come-down it must be for a woman of her background to end her days in this dump of a place – well, it can't have been her first choice. Trudi, that fountain of all knowledge, tells me that it was a succession of punishing death duties which ultimately drained Sybil's family of their once large fortune, and that in later life Caspar, never more than a dilettante in business matters, had fared badly at Lloyd's.

Through her wistful grey-green eyes set in an oval face Sybil notices me looking at her, a faint smile playing about her pretty-old-girl lips beneath her fine, delicate powdered nose with the wide, thoroughbred nostrils, her silver hair drawn up in a sort of twenties'-style bun. 'How is your back behaving?' she asks me nicely.

I tell her what a help my support, my corset, is proving to be. It gives me much more confidence in myself when I walk around.

'Perhaps we should all wear one,' she says. 'It might help our *posture*. Stop us sitting slumped all day in chairs. You know, when I was a girl I was made to sit straight in a chair with a ruler up my back. Mother was very strict about *posture*.'

The others stir in their chairs as if about to brace their shoulders back in the Edwardian manner.

'You sit up pretty straight now, Lady Sybil, if I may say so,' says knightly Tim Follaton, with warmth in his rustic voice and deference in his tilting head. 'Lesson to us all.'

This was true. Sybil always sits with a majestic mien, her head held high, from which, it could be said, it is the easier for her, a small woman, to look down her thin nose at the plebeian posturings of the rest of us.

'You are very kind,' she replies to Tim, at which he tilts his head again as if she has just dubbed her stooping knight.

'She's a very kind lady,' adds Megan Rees, mixing things up somewhat as she chases a runner bean round her plate with her fork, under which no doubt it will soon come to rest.

At which Ingrid Mackintosh snorts, either out of contempt or because she has a blocked nostril. You can never be sure with Ingrid. No one slouches in her country, she says, pronouncing it *slouschers* and meaning not Scotland but her native Germany.

Trudi and I, sitting side by side, laugh out loud together, though we try to make it seem as if we are sharing in the general jollity rather than at Ingrid's xenophobic intervention. Ingrid catapults a stony look at us across the table.

It is perhaps a little surprising that with all this chatter about straight backs and so forth our two ex-soldiers remain silent. But Bill looks bored to a frazzle, crunching away at his roast rib of pork, gravy dribbling down his chin, while Caspar sits looking vacantly in front of him, his vision probably a blur since, not for the first time, he has left his spectacles upstairs by mistake. He must be all too familiar with Sybil's party piece about the ruler up her back. Maybe he is thinking what a far cry is all this inconsequential drivel about posture from the sizzling repartee, the whinnying laughter, of his gallivanting youth, when he bounced along the Mall like a crown prince astride a shining black steed, his breastplate and plumed helmet bedazzling gawping bystanders with their glittering reflectors.

After lunch I join the others drifting from the dining-table into the sitting-room area, mainly to continue talking with Trudi, with whom I am developing an easy-going, conspiratorial sort of relationship. Conspiratorial in its intimacy, in the sense that when we are alone together we enjoy stepping outside ourselves to look back on or forward at life in general as well as to observe the fads and

foibles of our fellow-residents. We have too our link, however tenuous, with books and publishing, yet mostly we
manage to avoid talking shop. Trudi has no need to establish her credentials as a writer, and she has made only
occasional passing references to her pecuniary if not literary success. And we have this other link through her
erstwhile husband, Claud Schott, with whose Bohemian
pitch in Soho I was once loosely connected, drawn there
by various off-beat poets and writers whom the firm I
worked for elected to publish. It must have been about the
same time that I met Arabella, who had recently started
her career as a freelance photographer. In fact our meet-
ing took place at a small publisher's party my firm gave
for a writer whose photograph, reproduced on the dust-
wrapper of the book we were launching, had been taken
by her. We left the party together and remained so almost
uninterruptedly to the very end of her life.

I have spoken very little about Arabella to Trudi, and
she has asked me nothing about the circumstances of her
death, out of tact not indifference, though listening with
sensitivity to what, haltingly, I have confided in her. Of
course I have said nothing about my garden, that blue
evanescence beyond which I seek to wander in my dreams,
repeatedly retracing my steps, trying repeatedly to recapture the sequence of events that led to the extinction of
my beloved Arabella, to wrest them from the past as if
she herself were recoverable. Once when I was talking
about Arabella I suppose I became visibly upset. It was
that which prompted Trudi to look at me in her wise,
white owlish way and remark with her crackly voice: 'You
know, I think you blocked on mourning. You should let it
out, Mike. Let it right out.'

Now Trudi and I sink back into armchairs, sipping coffee. With my stiff corset I am better off, more comfortable, sitting upright; but never mind, I shan't stay here

long. For one thing the television has been switched on again. A huge set, it occupies a dominant place beside the fireplace which faces the entrance door, where it is left blaring and glaring at the occupants of the sitting area, whose chairs are positioned strategically more or less in a semicircle around it, as if it were some sort of shrine, for most of the day, with the exception of lunchtime. All the same, the residents seem to watch it periodically for only short spells, news bulletins and suchlike, the women either dozing or knitting or, as in the case of Ingrid, engaged in stitching a tapestry, such fingerwork supposedly helping to exercise stiff joints; while the men read their newspapers or large-print books. Often Caspar is the only male present, aside from occasional men visitors at the weekend, seated as ever dutifully beside his wife. He is there now, slightly flushed from his hot meal or reverie of bygone splendour and skirt-chasing, while Sybil stares disinterestedly towards the coloured screen, fondling her necklace which, dangling low over her bosom when she stands upright, lies bunched and shining like grapes in her lap. This remarkable adornment, which at first glance might be taken for a gewgaw, is composed of matching black pearls, the size of marbles. It transpires that they were given her as a present by King Zog when she visited Albania with her father between the wars. She calls them 'my Zoglets' and is never to be seen without them by day.

Now Trudi has decided to have a nap, so I get to my feet and cross the room to the side door. I think I shall go for a stroll in the village. Sybil looks up and throws me a gracious smile of encouragement, exposing the wrinkles round her neck like the rings inside a tree stem, and Caspar emits a chummy grunt, as I pass their chairs; but the others, already drifting into their post-prandial slumber, what they call 'forty winks' but which often extends to teatime, don't notice my departure.

9

There is a pinch of late autumn in the air as I set forth, and a tang of mulch from rotting plants and sodden leaves. The front gardens of the little houses have shed their blooms, their window-panes transmuting the pink and hazy sunlight as from a wizard's crucible into sheets of bronze. I take my usual promenade, round the stone war memorial at the far side of one end of the village and then back towards the church at the opposite end. The road is empty but for a tabby cat, which sidles up to me and strokes itself against my legs. I feel its glossy tail curling between my fingers, and then it meanders away. I walk stiffly like a clockwork toy soldier, its spring almost unwound, and carry my metal walking-stick in case I stumble.

I have gone only a hundred yards or so when I hear shouting, the sound grating against the still afternoon. I stop for a moment to listen, uncertain as to its source. It is quickly apparent that it is coming from the direction of the coach-house adjoining the nursing home, and the raised voices must therefore belong to the Durrances. They are doing more than exchanging words, to be sure, in fact they are having a blazing row, though they are too far away for me to be able to catch anything of what they are bandying at each other. It is not a happy sound and I have no desire to eavesdrop on them. I wish I hadn't heard any of it. So I continue walking, past the church and graveyard. There are only a few houses beyond,

46

succeeded by a group of bungalows set back, and then the narrow road, tall hedges each side, curves downwards and between fields of farmland towards the next village, some five or six miles away. I find it a hazard walking by the roadside beyond Saxton. There is comparatively little traffic at this time of year, but you can be confronted by an oncoming car very suddenly or, just as unpredictably, a motor vehicle can steal up on you from behind, at which you are forced to hug the side of the road tightly.

I am thinking these thoughts, not for the first time, when I hear the roar of a car accelerating at my back. I am walking, correctly, on the right-hand side of the road but the driver of the car, a black sedan, makes next to no allowance for me as he sweeps by, too fast for safety, smoke belching from the exhaust, and I have to grab hold of the hedgerow to avoid being struck. I have seen this vehicle quite often in the village and my eyes snap a vivid cameo of the driver, head bent forward, fierce face, his hands on top of the steering-wheel in the racing position.

Winded by this encounter and wishing to avoid another one with possibly the same car on its return run, I turn back towards the village. Shortly after I have passed the church I see lying on the right-hand side of the road facing me a little pile of fur. The animal is half on its side, showing the white of its stomach. My fear is confirmed when I recognise it as the cat that befriended me only a short while ago, its tail now limp, streaks of blood painting the tarmac beside its motionless body. It is quite dead. I am stabbed by a sharp sense of *déjà vu* as I bend down beside it, at which point Rosie Durrance crosses the road and walks up to me. She looks flushed, her hair is awry, her mouth half open.

'It's dead?' she mutters almost in disbelief.

I nod. 'Yes. It must have happened very quickly. It couldn't have suffered.'

47

'Bastard,' she says. 'The bastard.' Then after a pause she adds: 'I'm sorry, Michael, I shouldn't involve you in this, but you know who it was, don't you?... Denbigh. It was Denbigh who must have killed the cat.'

'Yes, I'm afraid so. He passed me down the road.' I gesture with a hand, indicating the direction. 'He was belting along – damn nearly got me too.' I say this with an attempt at a smile, not wishing to offend.

'Oh dear, I *am* so sorry. How awful for you.... I'll have to tell Mrs Price – about her cat. Poor woman, she was so attached to Curly. She'll be very upset. She lives at Number 3 – you know, one of the terrace cottages.'

'Yes, I know where you mean. I'll come with you if you like. Perhaps I should bring the cat. We can't very well leave him here.'

'Oh, would you? Bless you. Can you manage him?'

'If you could just take my stick.'

I bend down again, back straight, knees forward in the correct remedial manner, and pick up Curly, taking him in my arms. The body is still warm, the little tiger face untouched, his eyes shut as if he is merely asleep. We walk, our cortège of two, to Number 3 Orchard Terrace, where Rosie goes up the short stone path to the front door and rings the bell. I remain just outside the wooden gate leading into the front garden to give Rosie a chance to break the bad news to Mrs Price. I hear the door open and first Rosie's and then Mrs Price's voice. I can see Rosie has an arm round Mrs Price's shoulder. Then after a few minutes Rosie rejoins me and asks me to put Curly's body in a black bin-liner and leave him by a shed at the back of the cottage. When Mr Price returns from work he will bury the cat in the garden. Later Rosie tells me she offered Mrs Price reparation in any way that is appropriate, but Mrs Price won't accept anything. 'It was always a risk,' she told Rosie. 'Curly liked wandering and we couldn't stop him,

48

could we, cars and all?' None of them, including Curly, could have reckoned on the demonic driving of Denbigh Durrance, that's for sure.

'Would you like a drink?' I ask Rosie as we leave Orchard Terrace. 'At the Hereward?'

'That would be lovely,' she replies. 'It's just what I need. I'm not on duty again till this evening.'

'You work very long hours,' I remark, just for something to say, as we approach the Hereward Arms.

I have visited the pub only occasionally, in the hot weather for a chilled glass of lager, accompanied by Bill or Tim, but this is the first time I have been here with Rosie, or any of the nursing-home staff for that matter. Of genuine antiquity, the half-timbered building is now divided into two main sections for the public on the ground floor, the larger, barnlike one being used for the serving of food, while the smaller one is situated by the bar. It is a relatively unspoilt venue and the inevitable muzak is usually kept at a low volume except sometimes on Saturdays; in the summer for instance when the front door and windows are left open and you can then hear strains of it even in the back rooms of Saxton House, thumping away into the night. Rosie has mentioned it rather than complained to the landlord, but even so the din cannot be of any great concern to her, since most of her flock are quite deaf, apparently oblivious to the racket often belching non-stop from the television room, a sound that could be taken by a passer-by for a sort of geriatric rave-in.

There are a few people standing by the bar while the big room is virtually empty, so we decide to sit there in a discreet corner where we can't be overheard. I bring our drinks to the table: a large gin and tonic for Rosie, a brandy for me. We talk a bit about Curly, the impermanence of life, here today gone tomorrow kind of thing.

49

For a while there is some awkwardness between us, yet I feel that in this situation it is not for me to take the lead. The demise of the cat, sad as it is, a feline calamity, is a side-effect of a larger human drama, of which I caught uncouth strains nearly an hour ago as I was walking through the village.

'We had a terrible row, you know,' Rosie says suddenly. 'I mean me and Denbigh. I'm sure you must have heard us screaming at each other like a couple of fishwives – or do I mean banshees?'

'Yes, I did,' I reply. 'I think you may mean fishwives.'

Anyway the analogy is not only politically incorrect but singularly inappropriate.

'We haven't been getting on very well – God, not for weeks now. I won't embarrass you by going into the sordid details. I think it's partly to do with the fact that Denbigh hasn't really enough to occupy himself. Of course he's a back-up for me at the home. He's not interested in the running of the place, not one bit, but he does all sorts of maintenance jobs around and about you may not be aware of. And he also does nearly all the bulk buying and general fetching and carrying, but it's somehow not enough for a man his age. After all, he's not even fifty yet. I know he has his vintage cars, three of them now, which may not sound like much but they're as many as we can afford, quite apart from the limited space we have for them. And did you know about his model trains?' I shake my head. 'Well, he has a whole room put aside just for them. He spends literally hours there by himself, making them go round and round. He doesn't watch the telly, just gawps at these stupid trains. He's a regular trainspotter, that's what he is.... I'm married to a trainspotter! It's a small boy's hobby, as I've told him. And this mania for old cars is just another part of it.'

'Some men like collecting things,' I say, rather in

defence of the male sex than with much relevance. 'Maybe he's a subliminal curator of, well, a model museum. A curator *manqué*.' I say this also partly to play for time. I don't want to be drawn into the sexual aspect of the Durrances' relationship, which I sense could be at the root of their discord, trains or no trains. I imagine it often is in married lives. I don't want Rosie to blurt it all out and then regret it.

She pushes her head forward in that chicken-like way of hers. '*Manqué! Manqué?*' she ripostes. 'There's nothing *manqué* about Denbigh, what with his Railton, his Delage, his Riley – that's the one he killed the cat with, and almost one of my patients, too, by the sound of it. And God knows how many more trains he's got hidden away. Trains, trains, trains – his room, his not so little den, is stacked with *trains*. Museum curator? He's his own station-master as well. He's even got an old station-master's hat he puts on sometimes – can you imagine – and a whistle!' Rosie affects to laugh but looks wretched; then, changing her tone, she says: 'Here, let me get the drinks this time. Another brandy?'

When we have finished our second round of drinks, Rosie turns to me and says softly: 'Come back to the house with me – I mean my house. It's cosier there.' I make as if to decline the invitation but she presses me, 'to keep me company while I am feeling low,' she says.

On the way to the coach-house I notice for the first time a red mark on one side of her face, just above the cheek-bone, most of the make-up with which she tried to conceal it evidently having been absorbed by her skin. As I do so she touches the tell-tale spot with her hand, protectively. It looks swollen now, with a bruise already appearing.

I have never been in the coach-house before. There is a small entrance lobby for hanging coats and so on, and this leads into a spacious room, part of which is a hall/ dining-room and the other half, with an attractive brick fireplace, is the sitting area. A central staircase acts as a divider between the two parts. There are glazed chintz curtains each side, the large sofa and armchairs being covered with the same William Morris ivy pattern. I anticipated horse brasses and hunting prints everywhere, but the pictures are a pleasing mixture of nineteenth-century-style watercolours of gentle landscapes in thin gilt frames and some naturalistic contemporary oil paintings, mostly still lifes of fruit and flowers, while in an alcove by the staircase, tucked away like a disused calendar, there is an unframed poster of Marie Laurencin's sylphlike portrait of Coco Chanel which I know from the Louvre. Perhaps that is how the robust Rosie would like to look.

Rosie pauses in front of a looking-glass by the entrance lobby. 'My God I look a fright,' she says, straightening her hair with her strong, firm hands, the backs sprinkled faintly with freckles, and then examining her bruised cheek. I stand looking vaguely around and away from her. 'Now, let's drown our sorrows,' she adds, walking into the dining area. I follow her.

This part is in some disarray. For one thing, the long refectory table in the middle hasn't been cleared, of plates, cutlery and glasses. The remains of a recent meal are in evidence, too, as though it was suddenly interrupted. A stained, crumpled napkin lies on the floor. Rosie makes for a tray of drinks on a Welsh dresser at the far end of the room. 'Now, I wonder what we have in the way of brandy.... Ah, here we are.' She pours me a large measure in a wineglass and helps herself to an equally generous slug of gin. 'No tonic water? Oh well, I'll have it pink.' And she adds drops of angostura bitters to her glass, followed by some water from a jug on the dining-table. We take our drinks into the sitting-room.

'Now, Michael, where would you like to sit?'

I choose an armchair, a little too deep for comfort in my corset, while Rosie plonks herself heavily on the sofa with a long-drawn-out sigh.

Rather to my surprise, she doesn't launch into another diatribe against Denbigh, but asks me how I feel about life at Saxton House in general, and in particular how I see my future when I am fully recovered, that is to say when my leg and back have mended themselves. It is reassuring that she takes it for granted that I shan't be spending the rest of my days at Saxton House and I realise she is not prying, just showing genuine concern.

I tell her I am contented enough in the circumstances but that I can't help feeling fidgety, anxious to start a normal life again, though I am uncertain as to what I shall do, where I shall live and so forth. I don't tell her I find it hard to make plans by myself, how quickly lethargy overtakes me when I try realistically to look ahead.

We talk a bit about the other residents, or 'patients' as Rosie likes to call them. 'I can see you hit it off with Trudi Harrigan,' she says. 'She's quite something, quite a character. Very observant too.'

I mention our links in the past but do not elaborate.

Rosie says how much she admires 'gutsy Sybil' also, and how devoted Caspar is to her. 'And Ingrid?' she asks me.

'She doesn't set out to please exactly.'

'No. Poor Ingrid. She gives very little away – not that I want to be nosy. I just keep my eyes and ears open for those who want to confide in me.... But did you know she was orphaned in the war?'

I shake my head.

'Her family, by which I mean her mother and father and older sisters, were killed towards the end of the war when Berlin was bombed. Ingrid survived because she happened to have been sent to stay with friends in a safer part of the country, though nowhere was really safe by then. I don't know any more, but then Ingrid can be very uptight. I think she feels bitter about the war and, well, towards the British. Not surprising, really. Her husband Robert Mackintosh – he was quite a high-up in the Forestry Commission, you know – rescued her from virtual destitution. Life was terrible in Germany in those days. But Robert was twenty years older and from what Ingrid implies it wasn't a love-match, on her part anyway. I'm telling you this in confidence, though I expect you'll tell Trudi – if she doesn't already know about it.'

'Of course. No, I don't think Trudi knows any of this.'

Inside I regret being dismissive of Ingrid, put off as I have been by her rebarbative manner. Arabella was right when she said I was apt to be too perfunctory in my assessment of people who had no appeal for me or who got under my skin. Her criticism still holds true. I should have withheld judgement of Ingrid. What terrors must have visited her childhood; what fearsome spectres must inhabit her dreams.

We sit in silence for a while, drinking our drinks, Rosie having replenished our glasses again. Her neck has become increasingly pink, matching the colour of her face, and I too am feeling the effects of the brandy – at first soothing, now dulling my senses. Not so much, however, as to shield me from noticing the odd, searching look Rosie gives me when at last I stand up and announce that I think I must go. It is now past four o'clock and apart from anything else I am concerned that Denbigh will suddenly reappear. Certainly I don't want to risk being embroiled in his altercation or running battle or whatever it is with Rosie. No possible good could come of that.

I have just reached the entrance lobby and turned to say goodbye when Rosie, her speech now exaggeratedly slurred, says: 'Look, you've got blood on your jacket.'

54

Whereupon she puts both her hands against the stain, stroking it with plump fingers, and then in a gentle movement lifts them to my face and slips them round my neck, drawing my head close to hers. Simultaneously she presses her lips against mine and then thrusts her tongue into my mouth. I taste gin and saliva, smell the cohabitant fruit rising from her body. Removing her tongue she says, almost in a whisper: 'Darling.... Darling Michael. You've been very sweet and patient. The perfect gentleman.' Then in a tiny, little-girl voice, that unimaginably of a small girl up to her cranium in gin, she adds: 'Would the gentleman like a little pussy, a pussy with a bushy tail?'

'I ... well, as a matter of fact ... now you come to mention it,' I stammer. 'Digby ... I mean Denbigh.... It's getting late....'

My hesitancy speaks for itself: if I am being offered a love-nest, I am in no mind to play the opportunist cuckoo.

Rosie steps or rather lurches back a pace as though slapped by my clumsy rebuff, which is just too much for her to bear after being clobbered by her husband. 'Yes,' she says after a strangled pause, retrieving her normal, rather toneless voice from where momentarily she discarded it in Never Never Land. 'Denbigh.... You know he dotted me one ... I can't take much more of it – these awful tantrums.'

She looks sunken, collapsed, this chunky, half-sloshed woman swaying in front of me, with her purpling face and bashed cheek. Yet I know full well that the sooner I leave the coach-house the better. These are troubled waters, and who am I to risk paddling in their cross-currents?

Rosie sees me out, thanking me again for my company and pressing my free hand with one of hers, steadying herself against the doorway with the other.

I walk back up the short drive to Saxton House, soothed by the cool air. The downstairs lights are on, as inevitably is the television in the sitting-room where I am hoping to take tea today, though four o'clock is the usual deadline. After flushing my face with cold water in the men's room I put my head round the kitchen door and ask if someone can rustle up a cup of tea for me.

I sit at the dining-table where presently Little Jo brings me a pot of tea. Megan Rees and Tim Follaton are the only two now seated, with blank eyes, in front of the television beaming across the room. For once the volume is switched down so I can't overhear a word of what is being said by those participating in what seems to be a mixed discussion panel of five people, with a woman presenter seated at the centre, a small pile of books in front of her. They take it in turns, these all-wise eggheads or facile cuff-shooters, to motion with their hands in staccato, unnatural movements, either as if chopping meat on a block, winding balls of wool or playing cat's-cradle. For her part the eager, smiling presenter, vermilion-lipped, her yellow hair streaked with pink and frizzed out like Struwwelpeter in the fashion of the day, periodically raises both hands and tweaks her index fingers, presumably to indicate quotation marks.

As I watch from an angle the distorted, flickering figures with their jerky, tic-tac gesticulations, I begin to feel drowsy.... I cup my chin in my hands and close my eyes; no passion spent.

10

I have seen Rosie only intermittently in the past two weeks, clucking hither and thither, thrusting her head forward in little jerks. She has behaved in a friendly, perfectly normal way towards me, pretty well as she did before our tête-à-tête in the coach-house, for which I am thankful. I admire her sophistication and professionalism. Evidently Denbigh is back in the fold because the other day I saw his orange hatchback outside Saxton House while he was making one of his regular deliveries of provisions from the supermarket. Not surprisingly, the bruise on Rosie's cheek, ripening to purple and now faded to sepia, like a tea stain, has been the subject of some speculation among the residents, though only Trudi has guessed the truth of the matter, which she confided in me. I have told her about the cat being killed but not of my subsequent visit to the coach-house. The others seem to have accepted Rosie's explanation that she accidentally bumped against the open door of a kitchen cupboard. For their part the nurses have kept a respectful silence, which persuades me to think that they have reached the same conclusion, intuitively as well as from personal observation, as Trudi.

The residents, as well as Alice and one of the kitchen staff, have been suffering seasonal coughs and snuffles, which so far I have been lucky to escape. Ingrid is confined to her room with a bad cold, and Megan has a nagging cough which bothers her twofold, since she is concerned about keeping her bedridden roommate, Doris

Ashtead, awake at night. Sybil has told Caspar, one of the snufflers, to stop sniffing 'that horrid powdered tobacco', but for once he has ignored her, insisting that snuff helps clear his head, if not his mind, for he still contrives to forget where he has left his spectacles from one day to the next. Otherwise things have settled back more or less into their old grooves as the end of the year approaches.

Not so my dreams: I have had a recurrent nightmare. In this I find myself walking in the village. As I do so I pick up a cat (it has to be Curly), then fondle it until it leaps from my arms into the path of a passing motor car. I try to reach out and save it but the car knocks it over and careers on without stopping. There is blood on the road and blood on my hands as I lift up the dead animal. But now it is no longer the cat and instead I am holding Arabella, who looks up at me in that half-amused way of hers, her mouth curving in a smile. 'Thank God you're alive,' I say, at which she slumps lifeless, her head falling back. I kneel down with her and give her the kiss of life, trying desperately to revive her by the roadside. Soon I feel the body move and then the eyes flicker open. But they aren't Arabella's. It is Rosie who is lying there cradled in my arms.

It is the repetition that has turned this silly though vivid dream with its transmogrifications into a nightmare to be dreaded. I am trying deliberately to avoid it, to push it out of reach by adjusting my habits. For instance, instead of switching off my bedside light by ten o'clock, I stay awake an hour longer, sometimes two hours, reading. Or I make a mental list of places I should like to go and see when I am fully mobile. I think of touring Scotland, visiting the Western Isles, travelling in Ireland, my mind zigzagging along a network of arterial roads into open country.... I mean to disturb the pattern of my nights, close up any chinks through which this tedious new intrusion into my sleep may slither. For three or four days, or rather nights, the trick seems to be working, though for the time being I dare not revert to putting my light out at ten o'clock.

So it is with some relief that I find myself after an unaccountable lull drifting into the blue garden. I somehow sense that by its greater power and familiarity this prelude to my dream of dreams will superimpose itself upon the usurper and so cancel it out like the images in one roll of negative film pressed upon another. However, I cannot count on taking up automatically from where I left off the time before. Sometimes it is as if I press an alternative selection button on the remote control of a television screen and connect with a different channel from the one I was previously viewing. One night I am in Paris, the next in Rome. One minute I am walking through the grassy, flowered Jardin des Tuileries, another minute I am haggling over some trinket with a vendor standing by his souk under a baking sun in Marrakesh. Yet on occasions I do find that by thinking singularly, by sheer concentration, through a series of heaped-up and contained emotional impulses, I can reach a particular point in time; yet almost simultaneously, as I hinted earlier, I have to be looking the other way, so to speak, to relax my inner self, to rid my conscious state of the clutter of precognition. Krishnamurti says that when thought is silent there is emptiness, which is order; and it is through order in my dreams, and when my outer mind is quiet, that perhaps I may at last pluck the flower of resurrection.

Of course I cannot fool myself: I am uneasily aware of the exact spot towards which I am ever being drawn. Sooner or later I shall have to go through with it, to keep the appointment my subconscious has with destiny. I see the empty-faced, hooded reaper's cold raised finger and where ineluctably it is pointing.

*   *   *

And here I am again, retracing my steps in the familiar terrain. Shall I reach the end of the trail this time? Here we are, Arabella and I, walking side by side in the Jardin du Luxembourg. The panorama, the vista is unchanging, the same little incidents will continue to repeat themselves, the same figures will reappear, assuming their previous postures. I see the same smudged faces, the same kindly old women feeding the pigeons under the chestnut trees. They are as familiar as fellow-passengers in a ship or on a train, and just as those strangers can remain etched in one's memory for long afterwards, so have the inhabitants of my nightly travels taken up certain positions like sculptures in a museum or art gallery. Sometimes I remain stuck there, transfixed, because I fear moving on, and then, as soon as I find myself guiding Arabella towards one of the exits, I wake myself instantly as out of a nightmare when one finds oneself plunging over a cliff.

Not so today, the sun warm on our backs as we watch the steam rising from the carpet of drying leaves. Is it now, reminded as she is by the impermanence of life, that Arabella turns to me and says, 'I want to have a good death'? Is she advancing her demise by speaking like this? I wonder. Why does she go on so about death, about her death? She is still young, her sweet flesh is firm and smooth, her emerald eyes bright, she will have many more years by my side. And there are still so many places for us to explore, rivers to cross, horizons to enchant us. No, we shall never part.

'You won't ever leave me?' I half ask in response to her declared final aspiration. But inside I know that that isn't what she means at all. She is speaking surely of being at peace with herself at her life's ending, at the very end of the voyage. That is what is of deep concern to her.

'One must learn when to let go,' she says.

I am already dying a little at the merest hint of losing

her, as we meander out of the Jardin du Luxembourg. What is it that occurs on the Rue de Tournon, what rift in our communing, that causes us to shift from the sublime to the ridiculous? All I know is that we are having a crazy argument, our tinny, excited voices spiralling, at which passers-by crane their necks as though searching the air for an unidentified flying object. Is it, as I suspect more keenly each time I recite these events, yet another extension of that interminable wrangle about directions? For example, Arabella has a curious abhorrence of maps. She has no time for them at all. When we are travelling across Europe she often refuses to consult the map when I am driving and ask her which turning I should take. And when she does so she determinedly looks at the wrong section, or holds the map upside-down, or has the vapours – 'reading' when the car is mobile makes her feel sick, she says. I observe these evasive actions out of the corner of my eye: watch her way, endearing in retrospect, of fudging what she doesn't wish to do. And whereas I like to know exactly my position on the map at any given moment, like a lone sailor navigating dangerous reefs, she couldn't care less whether we are in Biarritz or Baalbek, as long as she is enjoying herself and the scenery. She is content simply to be guided by signposts and the look of a place regardless of its name or situation.

Am I consulting my street plan of Paris as we amble down the Rue de Tournon? Arabella hates me unravelling it in the street and, flinching as from a leper, invariably walks away when I do so, looking she says, like a dimwit tourist. I think this is unlikely here and now, since I know many of these streets, even their sometimes complex intersections, quite well. More probably I am concerned about the time, that unless we walk a bit faster we shall be late arriving at the restaurant where I have booked a table for lunch. Arabella has a cavalier attitude towards punctuality;

61

she seems to make a point of arriving late. She likes to remind me that it is bad manners for a guest to arrive on the dot. In contrast, as I believe I have already said, I am a slave to the clock. A serf indeed, manacled to maps and chained by time....

Are all movements related to one another or are they merely a series of isolated acts thrown together? Is each step we take dependent on the next and therefore any plan of action prone to capriciousness? If Arabella and I had not turned left where we did into the Rue St Sulpice, and with no good reason, had we instead pressed straight ahead, as was logical, and crossed the Boulevard St Germain into, say, the Rue de Seine, then taken the first turning right at the intersection of the Rue de Buci – or, alternatively, proceeded from the boulevard down that little alleyway, the Rue Grégoire de Tours, into the Rue Dauphine (you will have noted my obsession with directions) – we would have saved ourselves needless diversions and probably ten to fifteen minutes. Like a detective returning to the scene of a crime I went over the same ground many times, and at the end of each of these not so much sentimental as manic excursions I reached the same conclusion on the time element. It goes without saying that I haven't been able to reorder the flow of traffic precisely as it went on that fateful afternoon, but I have allowed minutes for delays of one kind or another.

None of these self-indulgent excursions had any point, save as a means of relentlessly chastising myself for not taking a grip of things at the outset. For I was now retreading ground where in fact Arabella and I never went in the first place. The crux of the matter was what occurred, or didn't occur, near the church of St Sulpice after the clock struck the hour.

* * *

One moment Arabella is there, the next moment she isn't. I look this way and that, cross and recross the square several times.- There aren't many people about and she will be easy enough to spot in her distinctive parrot-green suit, coruscating among the other pedestrians. But she is nowhere in sight. She has sprung this vanishing act on me so often; it is nothing new. We can be walking along chatting away and then suddenly I find myself talking not to Arabella but to a complete stranger. Sometimes this can be quite embarrassing, especially when I address the woman concerned as 'Darling' or 'My love' or 'Sweetheart', at which I receive a startled or aggrieved look as if I am trying to effect a pick-up. Of course this is less the case in Paris, where I might rather be taken for *un Anglais excentrique*. Most disconcerting of all is when Arabella crosses a street without any forewarning. Moreover she is an habitual jay-walker, seemingly quite heedless of traffic even in a city thoroughfare. Her vague if not wilful lurching into highways and byways, her frequent disregard of traffic signals, of little red men blinking a warning that you should not cross the road, can make me angry with her, not only because of the threat to her own safety but for the anxiety she causes me on her account. So, in one way or another, I am in permanent fear of losing her, in a permanent state of funk.

I have now reached the point when what I sometimes call my blue dream lets me down, or rather suddenly evaporates like a mirage in a desert place. For, in the Parisian context, it has never taken me past the Place St Sulpice on this day that is of such concern. What follows when I don't wake up instantly as the clock strikes like an alarm bell is a series of apparently unconnected diversions, the typical sort of muddle in which you can find yourself on so many disturbed nights. What instead I am always hoping for is that it may project upon the screen of my sleep that elusive route Arabella took when she disappeared.

The irony is that I can't recall which way I myself went after I left the Place St Sulpice. To put it mildly, I was in a terrible lather. Having blundered about looking in vain up and down various side-streets, I thought my best course was to head for the restaurant without more ado. I might spot Arabella on the way, or even find her there waiting for me. In the intervening years I have often challenged this decision. I might profitably have taken up a strategic position in the Café de Flore or the Deux Magots. But this is of course purely academic now. I believe I took as direct a route as possible for the river, for I remember I had to walk for ten minutes or more along the *quais* before I reached the restaurant.

It was almost exactly a quarter to two when I entered Lapérouse. I apologised profusely for being so late, saying something to the effect that I had arranged to meet Arabella but that we had failed somehow to connect. It was a feeble excuse but must have sounded plausible, for I was received with concern and consideration, my dilatoriness being gently brushed aside, with regret that *Madame* wasn't with me. Clearly Arabella hadn't contacted the restaurant herself in the interim, which I thought testily was the least she could have done. It was bad enough for her to have left me in the lurch. I was snapping at her in my mind out of sheer anxiousness.

I had little appetite, but the fish I chose as a main course was as delicious as ever and served in that courteous way the French at their best manage so well and so effortlessly. I didn't drink immoderately – an aperitif followed by a half-bottle of white burgundy, and at the end of the meal when he brought me coffee the head waiter presented me with a complimentary glass of cognac. I followed it with another; and then another.

I left Lapérouse after three o'clock and headed for the hotel. There was a good chance that Arabella had had a snack somewhere and then retreated there. I felt mollified by the good food and drink I had consumed and was ready to apologise for upsetting her. We could make it up and enjoy the rest of our last day in Paris together, have dinner at a good bistro and then make love. We could soon put the contretemps of the morning behind us.

Arabella wasn't at the hotel but the girl at the reception desk told me she had been in earlier. It seemed she had left the hotel foyer a while before three o'clock, when I was lingering on at Lapérouse. I went upstairs to our room straight away. It was a small attractive room overlooking a quiet courtyard, with coral-coloured flock wallpaper and white furnishings. It had a comfortable double bed facing a table to one side with a television set, a built-in cupboard and a little glass-topped dressing-table, as well as two white wicker chairs. There was a line sketch of rooftops in a silver-leaf frame above the bed and a black-and-white drawing of a nude woman at the far end of the room. On the other wall, beside a louvre door leading into the bathroom, hung a Cocteau lithograph – a twirly profile of a head with a snail-shell eye, the arched eyebrow curling upwards like the antenna of a butterfly. Arabella's scent hovered in the air. Her hairbrushes were askew on the dressing-table and there was a light imprint on the pink padded bedcover, suggesting she had sat there for a moment. Then I saw the note, on a folded slip of paper on my bedside table. It read: *AT DM – A*. So she must have departed for the Deux Magots nearly an hour ago.

I left the hotel without delay and set off down the Rue Jacob. I walked briskly, with the happy thought that all was forgiven. Arabella's succinct note had confirmed as much by inviting me to meet her at the café. She had always liked it there, she had known it since her student days at the Sorbonne, but it was not my favourite haunt by any means. It seemed to me to depend too much on its associations with famous figures of the past, writers and so forth; and on that account perhaps the waiters were sniffy, expecting immediate payment for whatever one consumed. And as for watching the world go by, well, these days St-Germain-des-Près seemed to be peopled largely by young tourists almost indistinguishable in jeans and trainers, or frumps in trouser suits. Fashionable passers-by were few and far between. A painter with Caillebotte's eye for elegance, for the measured stride of the hatted and umbrella'd, for dappled rays silvered and refracted by folds of rustling dress or frock-coat, for a gentleman's proffered arm, his lady's dalliance, might have been at a loss. Yet it was still a good meeting-place and if you sat there long enough and drank more than a token cup of coffee, the waiters became more tolerant if not altogether accepting of your custom.

I turned left at the Rue Bonaparte and had just passed the Rue de l'Abbaye when I saw Arabella diagonally to the right on the far side of the street, past the central island. She was either waiting for me or had just left the Deux Magots. She saw me immediately and waved, her green arm going back and forth in a quick, eager fanlike motion. I didn't see exactly what occurred next. She seemed to start running towards me still waving her arm, running across the street. At one and the same moment there came the sound of a single extended blast of a motor-car horn and a screech of brakes. A stream of cars on my side of the island continued rushing by, momentarily obscuring my view. Then through a gap I could see that a silver vehicle had stopped at the other side of the street and a number of pedestrians were already circling round it. There was no sign of Arabella.

I waited for the lights to change, for there was still an intervening line of traffic, and then in swift strides crossed the street, heading for where I had last seen Arabella, my heart thumping wildly. I pushed my way through the group of people standing by the stationary motor car and there I saw her lying in a pool of blood by the kerbside. Someone was trying to support her head and then two policemen appeared. I dropped down beside her and held her limp body in my arms, the blood soaking her green suit now smearing my hands, my sleeves, my jacket. Her face was ashen, filaments of her fine black hair falling across it and over her half-closed eyes, now drained of colour, while her crimson mouth hung agape in a look almost, I fancied, of astonishment. A policeman knelt down beside me and I heard him ask me as though from some other world to which I did not belong if I knew the dead lady.

'C'est ma femme. C'est ma femme, monsieur.'

The two policemen were joined by two others who dismounted from their motor cycles, and then several more arrived on the scene. Soon the place was teeming with policemen. They had started hand directing the traffic and one was questioning the driver of the obstructing car which had killed Arabella, making notes on a pad. The driver, a clean-shaven young man in his twenties, looked grey-faced and distressed, bewildered by his sudden notoriety. French motorists treat pedestrians like dumb hedgehogs, making them scurry from their path or be squashed flat. However, in this case the driver could have had no chance of avoiding Arabella, who must have stepped straight into the front wheels of his car, distracted when she spotted me approaching.

Quite a throng of people had now gathered and the

police began to push them back and instruct them to move on. Then an ambulance arrived, its clarion siren punching the air with its strident refrain. This activity was happening all around me, yet I could scarcely believe any of it, that it was anything to do with me, while I continued to hold my dearest one protectively as if I might still be able to rescue her from this madness, as if I could stave back the events unfolding around us like a terrible waking dream.

Two men eased Arabella's body on to a stretcher, covering it with a blanket, and then they lifted her into the ambulance. I climbed in and squatted alongside her, holding one of her cold hands in mine, pressing my face against her blooded cheek and then kissing her on her lips in what may have been a final desperate attempt to revive the passion they had so often yielded to me. When eventually I eased my head back, her precious face sagged apart from mine in that way of blank rebuff in which at the last the dead always spurn the living.

11

The days and weeks that followed remain confused and blurred in my memory. I suppose subconsciously I have tried continually to push them, along with other uncomfortable memories, into a dark void into which I need not venture again. In this I have been partly successful. But the void remains; I sense a hollow inside me, a deep cavern in which sorrow lies coiled like a watchful viper, ready to inject its venom into my bloodstream, penetrate my heart. No doubt this is what my friend Trudi had had in mind when she said I have blocked on mourning. I have deliberately shut it away. I have never allowed it to run its full course, never allowed the snake to slide out of its hiding-place into the open where eventually its poison would dry out, just as its skin would shrivel up in the dogday sunshine of reality.

A grim photograph of the accident appeared in *Le France-Soir* of Arabella sprawled on the street, a dark patch oozing from her, policemen in the background. The caption read: *Mort d'une photographe distinguée, de nationalité franco-anglaise, renversée par une voiture*, or words to that effect. It was accompanied by a short piece about Arabella's photographic work, which it affirmed had recently been exhibited in a prestigious Paris gallery. There was also a terse reference to Arabella in *Le Monde*.

Of course I had to pick myself up and pull myself together, and I telephoned various people to inform them of the tragedy, including Madame Duvivier, Arabella's widowed aunt who lived in the city, and my son Pip (Arabella's stepson) in London. I asked Pip to circulate the news among close friends in England, some of whom gathered for the funeral which took place a few days after the accident, Pip and his wife Daphne among them.

Arabella was essentially a spiritual person but not an adherent of any formal religion, so no hymns were sung and no prayers as such intoned by those gathered there, though Pip read a prayer of John Donne's. I recited two poems – by Lorca and Edward Thomas – which I knew by heart, as well as reading some passages from Krishnamurti's *Meditations*, a copy of which Arabella had left by her bedside; while Colette Munro, the proprietor of a London gallery where Arabella's work had been shown, and also a close friend, read on 'the secret of death' from *The Prophet*. Finally, I arranged through Jeanne Duvivier, herself a musician, for a violinist and cellist to play the *andante un poco mosso* of Schubert's Trio No. 1 in B Flat Major, a pianist already being available at the crematorium chapel.

A jarring note, for me at any rate, was struck by Henri Duvivier, son of Jeanne and Arabella's first cousin, who without forewarning stepped in front of the aisles at the very end, when to all intents and purposes the ceremony was over, and gave what purported to be an address. He spoke entirely in French, without deference to the pre-dominantly English-speaking gathering, although he was fluent in their language. And it was less an address or eulogy than an interminable reminiscence of childhood days he had spent with Arabella, in which I thought he seemed to feature more than did his young cousin. (I recall Arabella having told me that when she was in her late teens Henri had asked her to marry him, but, what-ever the bar of their blood relationship, she had never fan-cied him in romantic terms.) Henri, usually a cold, aloof

70

man, in my experience a somewhat typical Parisian of a certain well-heeled, well-manicured kind, was visibly moved by the proceedings, blowing his nose loudly and wiping his eyes with a large puce-coloured handkerchief throughout, as if overtaken by a virulent head cold. I found his demonstrative emotions at close quarters a distraction, as though he had appropriated for himself the role of chief mourner.

Certainly it was an emotive and sentimental occasion, and though given more time I might perhaps have ordered things rather differently (though I could hardly have anticipated Henri's artless peroration), I had, by assisting the quiet flow of tears from some of those whom Arabella had loved and cared for, helped unite us all in our grief.

Afterwards Madame Duvivier invited everyone back for tea and refreshments at her small apartment, crammed with antiques, paintings by friends and other works of art, on the Boulevard Voltaire. Somehow we managed to squeeze into it, including the three musicians who with those haunting Schubert cadences had plucked at our heart-strings, in what became a bibulous gathering, of which I remember practically nothing as I got quite drunk on an unchecked mixture of sparkling wine and Armagnac.

Pip tried very sweetly then, before eventually we all tottered out into the street in the early evening, and several times during the succeeding weeks, to persuade me to come to London to stay with him and Daphne in their house for a while. Colette, too, offered me a temporary haven in her Chelsea flat. But I couldn't bring myself to leave Paris, to which I now felt inextricably bound by ties of love and death as well as its many nostalgic associations which had drawn Arabella and me back there so often. Perhaps it was then, the pang of separation fossilising in our last shared moments, that my subconscious was already at work, secretly fashioning the blue garden

71

behind or beyond which Arabella's footsteps would forever echo in my dreams.

Soon I had the task of disposing of Arabella's ashes, which I had requested be handed over to me. I had decided to scatter them in the Seine – not a holy river like the Ganges, admittedly, but one of beauty and romantic persuasion that has flowed into verse and song.

I got up in the early hours one morning and took the casket holding all that was left of Arabella down to the Pont des Arts. We had usually crossed the river by this bridge on our way to the Louvre and elsewhere. It was cold and misty and the water below was grey, ribboned by darker ripples. There was no one about and no traffic to speak of. A single gull sat perched on the stone parapet, where it observed me with a glassy yellow eye. I shooed it away, unwelcome Nosy Parker, in case it mistook the contents of the casket I was about to disperse for a windfall *petit déjeuner*. I was thankful the air was still.

I opened the casket and looked for a moment at the powdery flakes inside, all that was left of the body I had cherished and held in my arms and entered in ecstasy. I took a handful and threw it over the parapet, careful not to drop any on the pavement. And then I clutched another and another handful and cast each downwards until there was a little snow-white cloud hanging there. When they reached the water some of the ashes floated on the surface for a while in spumelike slivers until they were absorbed by the grey-black current. Then I threw the casket into the river and muttered a blessing.

I believe as I walked away from the Pont des Arts on that drear, chill morning, that I had never felt so utterly alone.

12

For the next six months I rented a tiny apartment on the Rue des Cendriers in the 20th *arrondissement*. This came about through Jeanne Duvivier, who was a friend of the owner. The latter had left Paris to stay with relatives in the Languedoc region in southern France.

To begin with I was pleased to have a base of my own, and I paid only a peppercorn rent for it, but after a time I began to feel displaced there. It was not a part of the city I had known before and with which I could now identify. I have always relished the feeling of anonymity one has in unfamiliar places, particularly in foreign cities, but there is a difference between deliberate choice and force of circumstances. Naturally I ventured forth, but I avoided my old haunts on the Left Bank, regularly strolling instead in the nearby park and exploring Père Lachaise, which I had not done previously, situated as it was within easy walking distance of my apartment. Death was still uppermost in my mind and in a way I felt comforted contemplating some of those memorialised in the hallowed ground. Arabella hadn't believed in an afterlife or reincarnation and there was nothing of her left on earth to mark the simple fact of her existence. The Seine had swallowed her, as I believe she would have liked: she believed passionately in the transience of the human body, that it should perish without fuss like a flower. And yet I sometimes wondered if, metaphysically, the dead can reach heaven through the memory of others, of loved ones they have left behind. If that were so, Arabella would surely be circling the firmament where our riven hearts had sent her. A sentimental notion maybe, but one I had to contemplate if not enjoin were I to speak to her, which I now found myself doing unwittingly – in the street, on a bus, even in shops with people bustling about. Heads turned, I encouraged looks of curiosity, hostility, occasionally bemused sympathy. I ignored them, turned my back on them. Uppermost in my mind was my need to consult Arabella, to confide in her certain observations I had made, just as I had done when she was alive. And I found I could do so quite naturally if I envisaged her shadow by my side. I had to accept the absence of laughter that had magicked our days, but not so the inability to share my thoughts any more.

I took trouble preparing meals for myself in my little perch on the Rue des Cendriers. It helped me occupy some of the long slack days when I tired of reading or just wandering about. I didn't attempt anything elaborate but chose my provisions with care. French markets with their succulent offerings are such a joy, and there was an excellent one twice a week at the end of the street, extending three Métro stops along the boulevard. There fruit was piled high in gleaming pyramids; vegetables of every shape and variety lay snugly side by side like multicoloured candies; arrays of fish were presented in spangled mosaics; cuts of meat were ordered into neat red ranks with regimental exactitude, a whole pig at the centre of one display, complete with a lemon in its mouth and a crown of artichokes, like the commander-in-chief of a great army saddled amid his splendid battalions; and everywhere there were cheeses, yellow, blue, cream, orange, in rounds, squares or sausage-shaped, aromatic, tempting, inviting.

I became an habitué of this market: for me it was a feast for the eyes as well as a social centre. I enjoyed especially the company of the stallholders, who seemed genuinely interested in my simple repasts, offering me tips and helping me with my selections. They called me *Le Gentilhomme*, a complimentary appellation, and I came to learn the names of my favourites among them. They were my friends and I missed sorely their welcoming smiles, their kindly red faces and gravelly voices when I moved away.

It grew bitterly cold in March and I became more reclusive, hugging the electric fire for long spells in my snug bed-sitting-room. Arabella used to say that she would like to be a tortoise and hibernate in the winter, and I fancied that, had she believed in reincarnation, I might if I rummaged imaginatively rediscover her, with a beautiful shell on her back, tucked in a nest of straw in a pet shop somewhere. I was sure I would have recognised her at once by a certain look in her eye, a tell-tale gleam.

I now wondered if I had made a dreadful mistake lingering on in Paris. I had no friends of my own and Jeanne Duvivier, my only family contact with whom I had an affinity, had left the city to stay with friends of hers in the Midi during the winter months. Yet I couldn't quite bring myself to go back to England, where I feared I might feel even more out on a limb than I had begun to feel here. I had made only one trip across the Channel since the funeral, to collect some more clothes and arrange the letting of my house. Then I went back at once to Paris.

When the time came for me to quit the Rue des Cendriers, the owner having returned from the South, I was lucky to find a pleasant, if scruffy, studio apartment with a moderate rental on the Rue du Bac, within a stone's throw of the river. It suited my needs and my mood. I now wanted once again to walk the streets I knew and loved so well. Pip came to stay with me for a few days, to 'keep an eye' on me as he put it, *en route* for a business trip in Reims and the champagne country. He had never cared much for Paris and so I set out to try to please him, introducing him to various art galleries and the modest restaurants I liked best which he hadn't previously visited. He reiterated his offer to me to stay with him and Daphne in London. But he could see for himself I was in no mood to abandon my old territory so soon after I had realighted there, and I may even have convinced him, such was my simulated buoyancy during his visit, that I was coming to terms with living alone.

It was during this spell, the warmth of spring rekindling my body, that I began to retrace the steps Arabella and I had taken on that fateful day those long, bleak months ago. But I didn't stay confined to the Left Bank. I crossed and recrossed the river many times. Yet wherever I was I seemed to search continually for Arabella, as if I could somehow will her back into a living entity. Fortifying my fantasy, I kept seeing her in shops and places we had visited together. Once I saw her in the Beaubourg. She was on the elevator, encased in that intestinal perspex worm in which you climb up the mesmerising, gutlike edifice to the main gallery. I raced after her, but she disappeared before I could reach her. Then, looking down from an upper viewpoint, I saw her again, standing outside watching one of the crowd-pulling buskers, this one chalk-faced, bowler-hatted, with a cane and baggy trousers, miming a mechanical Charlie Chaplin. But by the time I reached the place outside where I had seen her, she had gone.

Another time I saw her from behind in the Métro, mounting a train, but the automatic door shut in my face as I was about to follow her inside. And then I spotted her entering an art gallery by the Avenue Matignon where we had once bought a Matisse lithograph. I could tell by the shape of her head, the way her glossy hair was combed back over her neat shells of ears, by her unmistakable rolling gait, that it was Arabella. So I ran quickly after her and rang eagerly at the locked, heavy glass entrance door. I was out of breath as I entered and the steel-grey coiffured woman who let me in greeted me frostily if not with suspicion. The person I had pursued stood with her back to me, looking at one of the paintings displayed on the russet hessian wall. She gave me a queer twist of a smile, almost in imitation of Arabella, before stepping aside into the adjoining room. I thought for a moment of following her, making some comment or other about one of the pictures on display and then maybe inviting her for a cup of coffee. The old routine. But then I thought better of it, fearing polite rejection, and besides my heart was already turning again to stone.

In the next few months I had two or three more encounters in the street with so-called lookalikes. These were reminiscent of those times in the past when Arabella had done one of her vanishing tricks and I had found myself chatting up a total stranger, and yet again I felt slapped in the face by an all too typical *Anglais excentrique* look of dismissal, staunching the pitter-patter of my racing heart.

Unwittingly I began to ponder how much longer I could continue living this non-life of tramping the streets and drinking endless cups of coffee by myself, always on the lookout, always half conceiving that Arabella would suddenly and naturally reappear round the next corner, or the next, as though she had been only temporarily indisposed. I thought of those women I had successively approached or accosted, from whose faces Arabella's visage seemed to have been stripped off like a mask the moment they revealed their own identity. And I rehearsed over and over the last seconds I had seen her waving at me in the Place St-Germain-des-Prés as if I could draw comfort from the immortality in the image of her running to her death. That hectic movement of her arm, the fan-like waving of her hand, had been at one and the same time a signal of greeting and her last adieu.

Exactly a year to the day after Arabella died I went back to the Jardin du Luxembourg. Unlike the weather on that fair morning, it began raining heavily. I skirted the pond and then retreated for shelter beyond the terrace from where we had looked down and watched the scene around us, but today there were few people about and they were not drifting along but moving hurriedly, some shielding themselves from the torrent with umbrellas. Perhaps it was the sound of the rain hissing through the falling leaves, the sight of the grey, scurrying figures retreating from view like migratory birds, that epitomised for me the end of a season, an era, my dying hopes and dreams, the irrec-oncilability of the present with the past. A great and over-whelming sense of sadness swept through me and I began to weep.

And it was while I stood there sobbing beneath the dripping chestnut trees, the chill rain streaking my face, joining my warm tears in a gentle stream, my solitary fig-ure like a gaunt shadow of itself, as of a ghost waiting re-entry into the spirit world, that I first caught sight of my guardian angel. She was running. She was running in quick, urgent strides, a trail of spindrift behind her, splash-ing across the grass directly towards me.

AFTER

Cherish pity, lest you drive an angel from your door.

William Blake, *Songs of Innocence*

1

My mother used to say you must open your front door when midnight has struck on the last day of December to let the New Year in. I suppose this is one of those old superstitions like turning the silver in your pocket when you first spy the new moon, of which of course you should have a clear sight unobstructed by glass. At Saxton House we didn't see the New Year in communally, the residents having been tucked up at the usual early hour, and I am certain the front and back doors remained firmly shut, but I lay awake in bed and listened in the dark to the twelve chimes ring out from the village church.

Christmas, extraordinarily enough my second in the home, was a bit tedious with the forced jollity, the creaking camaraderie, though Rosie and the nurses, not to mention the kitchen staff, went to a good deal of trouble on our behalf to make it a truly seasonal affair. They dressed up the sitting-rooms with paper chains and glitter and balloons, and there was a large fir tree placed near the foot of the stairs in the entrance hall, blinking with fairy lights, which gave out a pleasant smell of pine. We sang carols on the morning of Christmas Eve, presided over by old Father D'Arly, Rosie thumping out the tunes with her strong hands on the yellowing keyboard of the upright piano at one end of the large sitting-room. Sybil must have been an accomplished soprano: though wavering somewhat on the higher notes, her voice still has touches of pure clarity. And Tim's rich baritone is especially pleasing to the ear with that attractive West Country intonation of his.

We had a good traditional lunch on Christmas Day and then pulled crackers with each other, helped by the nurses, who insisted on our wearing the paper hats which dropped out. I thought it was a bit like papering over the cracks of our crumbling lives.

For presents, we gave a huge box of chocolates to the nurses, with a round robin of cash, and a bottle of port and one of sherry to Rosie, intended partly for Denbigh as well, though in the event that proved to fall a little flat. Each of us residents was in turn given a jar of home-made strawberry or raspberry jam and a jar of plum pickle, made locally, mine tagged with a lucky charm of what seems to be an elf. I have put it by my bedside just as I might have done as a small boy when I hoarded ephemera of all kinds, such as those silver threepenny bits and horseshoes you would find hidden like nuggets in the Christmas pudding.

The weather – well, it's something to mumble about at lunchtime – has been relatively clement and the residents all seem to be quite fit, Megan having at last got rid of her nagging cough, and even Ingrid seems quite perky. The other day I heard the piano being played softly, in contrast to Rosie's boisterous accompaniment of our carol singing, and much to my surprise I found Ingrid seated there. She was playing the slow movement of a Beethoven sonata. For a while I sat alone unobserved and listened, and I felt quite moved both by the music itself and by this unobtrusive expression of Ingrid's hitherto unrevealed talent. When she stopped and moved away from the piano, a good deal less adroitly than she had played it, she saw me sitting nearby but seemed unperturbed by my presence. I told her how delicately I thought she played. She nodded and then looked at her hands and said they were no longer supple enough for her to attempt the other movements. 'I am better with the tapestry,' she added with a rare hint of a smile. I said I hoped that, even so, I could persuade her to play again another day, as I should much like to listen to her. In reply she said she might 'try a little Schubert', though presumably she would have to play from memory, the selection of musical scores at the home being somewhat limited. I said she should speak about this to Rosie, who I was sure would wish to encourage her to play. I recognise it as one of her strengths that Rosie is always trying to think up ways of providing the residents with some ongoing interest, at best a new stimulus, in their restricted lives. She thinks of even the oldest among us as individuals with something to give and not simply as recalcitrant children to be marshalled crocodile fashion and forced to toe the line as once I had unfairly concluded.

Meanwhile Rosie's own life has been thrown into a turmoil. At some point over the Christmas period, though exactly when we may never know, Denbigh made off with a girl from the village. Rumour has it that she was a barmaid at the Hereward Arms, a blonde girl still in her twenties, quite attractive too it is said and 'Flighty as they come', though that sounds like a cynical afterthought. 'Flighty she came and flighty she left,' said a local wag. Even so, what she saw in Denbigh remains something of a mystery.

This contretemps has exposed Rosie to a lot of extra work in the way of fetching and carrying, and she has had to summon additional help to keep supplies flowing steadily to the home, quite apart from the emotional travail she must have been caused. Of course during that visit of mine to the coach-house she had let slip the unhappy state of her relationship with Denbigh, in fact she mocked him bitterly, and so her present predicament was surely always on the cards. Yet on that occasion Rosie hadn't suggested that Denbigh was a philanderer, a Lothario figure; rather that he had somewhat puerile hobbies and a nasty temper he couldn't control. In other words, on the evidence, one can't make two plus two into six, and I don't feel inclined to try.

None the less the elopement has had a certain stimulating effect on our lunchtime gatherings. In fact the air has been abuzz with speculation about it. It continues to astonish me how scurrilous, or plain bitchy, the elderly can be. What conjectures must be made as soon as one's own back is turned? Yet perhaps I am just as prone as the others to scabrous comment, of which the following, yesterday, far from being a brisk exchange, as it may seem from the way I am recording it, spanned almost the whole of our repast, is an example. Who said what is immaterial.

'Where do you think Mr D has taken his little titbit?'

'We say *tidbit* in the States – it's considered more genteel.'

'Perhaps he's going down the Amazon?'

'Or up it.'

'Why the Amazon?'

'Wishful thinking ... well, it's a long way away and with any luck he'll get lost.'

'They're more likely to be in Clacton-on-Sea or Budleigh Salterton, if you ask me.'

'Did he set forth in one of his vintage models, do you suppose, the French one might be appropriate in the circumstances, or in that ginger Japanese number?'

'Always looked like vomit to me.'

'He's a reckless driver, I'm told. Ran over a cat in the village last year. Do you remember that nice tabby which used to wander in here?'

'That sort of thing appeals to some women. You know, speed, flash, fast cars, that sort of thing.'

'Women? Apparently the unfortunate girl in his clutches is young enough to be his daughter...'

'They've never had children, the Durrances, have they?'

'Maybe Mr D is impotent.'

'Important?'

'I-m-p-o-t-e-n-t.'

'Well, in that respect at least Rosie can be counted fortunate.... Be a dear and pass me the sugar, would you?'

'Sorry, dear. You do have a sweet tooth, don't you?'

'Fangs, my dear. Fangs.'

Megan looked puzzled but not discomposed by this self-mocking quip, Sybil sugaring it with a serene smile while ladling white granules on to her apple charlotte with a knotty hand, her cat's eye ring circled by cabochon diamonds catching fire in a sudden thin shaft of sunshine. I imagined her hand sparkling on the shoulder of a dancing partner as he whisked her elegantly around some grand ballroom in the halcyon days of her youth.

It is always 'Mr D' with the residents, never Denbigh. But this is probably due to the fact that he never troubled to make himself known to any of us. Rather he seemed to do his best to avoid us, and when on the few occasions I myself encountered him face to face he barely grunted 'Morning' or 'Afternoon' before scuttling on as if to escape bad breath or a gas leak. In contrast, there has been a strong wave of sympathy towards Rosie, who still goes about her work in her usual brisk and efficient manner. However, though she is putting on a bold face, affecting that nothing untoward has occurred in her life, I sense an edginess in her not apparent before. This comes out in various ways: it is not so much any subtle change in her facial expression as one of emphasis in her movements. There is something now of an automaton, of remote control in her body language, and an absent, dull look in her eyes, the hazel irises muddied.

In spite of our moments of intimacy in the coach-house last autumn I am loath to broach the subject with Rosie of Denbigh's defection. I think it is up to Rosie to speak to me about it if she feels so inclined. Yet I rather hope she doesn't, which is cowardly of me I dare say, but I fear it could place me on the edge of a slippery emotional slope, over which I might easily be tugged by compelling strands of pity or simple curiosity. There is little doubt in my mind that Rosie is suffering from sexual tension, in which she might be tempted to reach out for some handy means (i.e. me) of relieving it. I know she was drunk when she implanted her tongue in my mouth like a bee diving for pollen, but French kisses are French kisses whatever the condition of their executants and I suspected she had already taken a shine to me before that strange afternoon. Therefore I must be all the more careful now not to appear to encourage her when she is doubly vulnerable, with Denbigh well out of sight if not out of mind. It is odd for me to find myself playing the monk, but I am helped in my endeavour by a simple expedient: I still have to wear a corset which, by restricting me physically, has the function of a kind of monastic garment of restraint. In short, I am not yet ready, whatever the prospects, to fulfil the role of lover. Moreover, were I to surrender to the charms of the Principal, my place at Saxton House would soon become untenable. So it is that at night I cock my ears, apprehensive that I may hear stealthy footsteps outside my door.

2

It is March and already there is a touch of spring in the air. So far it has been unusually warm and daffodils are coming out of bud by the front drive and in the back garden, alongside clusters of primroses swaying like choristers with ruffs. Soon they will be joined by tulips, tall, orderly lines of red and yellow like ranks of infantry parading in a tattoo. I watch the seasons come and go through my bedroom window with a comfortable sense of detachment. A queer sort of paralysis has descended on me the more I have become absorbed into my surroundings. These days the world I left behind seems more remote than ever and my urge to return to it, so insistent over many months, has receded. My present lethargy has pushed aside all the resolutions I made to change things, to live differently, just as soon as I am truly fit again. In fact the stronger I have become physically, the less has been my wish to challenge the restrictions my infirmity has placed upon me. It is true that I am still prone to boredom, from which my chats with Trudi remain an often delightful release, but this is more a matter of a temperamental defect than of thwarted desires. And I tell myself that my new-found contentment, if evasive of the future, is at least preferable to the unreality of wishing things back as they were.

This shift of outlook is not accidental. I have brought it about through my own determination to explore the pain and perplexity of the tragedy that has afflicted me: the sudden death of Arabella. For a long spell I was unable to come to terms with my grief at her loss. While I was forced to recognise her death as a cold fact, I refused to contemplate life without her, notwithstanding the interposal of subsequent events, other relationships. The irreconcilability of these twin though disparate strands steered me into territory beyond the grasp of pure reason. As I have been at pains to illustrate, I was driven to seek solace in dreams. In these I hoped to recapture the joy of my union with Arabella, and as the nightly transfigurations intensified I came to think of her as always being within the circumference of a certain part of Paris, her footfall ricocheting along the streets we had trodden together. This fixed and unvarying idyll had its own attraction, and at first I was content to find myself in the same place, again and again, refocusing the blur of images I had held in my subconscious. For instance the couples trailing round the pond in the Jardin du Luxembourg, the women feeding the pigeons, the students seated languidly in chairs like passengers on the sun-deck of an ocean liner. This was a remission, lifting me from the emptiness of my days, relieving me of the pressures of loneliness. However, it proved to be only a temporary respite. Although to start with I had looked forward to re-engaging with the past by slipping through the mediatory veil I call my blue garden, I came to detect that all the while I was unwittingly edging towards a vale of sorrow. Now, wrested from my reverie of happy climes, I became locked in a restless search of revived locations for the person I had lost, scratching for clues as to what might have occurred if certain patterns had not been disrupted, if the final catastrophe could have been averted by, say, the simple resource of one or both of us engaging in an alternative topic of conversation. I kept thinking if only we could have avoided that footling quarrel at a particular spot, our attention might not have been diverted from where we were originally heading. In these perambulations time became all-important; yet because of the subliminal nature of hindsight acquired in sleep, time was out of joint. Whatever adjustments I might attempt in a replay of past actions, I couldn't put the clock back.

I began to realise that repeated recitation, my effort subconsciously to revive the last few hours of Arabella's life, merely led to a cul-de-sac, a blank wall over which I was unable to scramble. I grew more and more desperate in my yearning, tangible to me though futile, to cross the frontier of the unknown, to find out where precisely Arabella had gone when she wandered off in the Place St Sulpice, so that even now I could pursue her and hold her back from the abyss. Yet however unacceptable was the obvious in my dreams, I awoke with the mundane recognition that you cannot report back from a land, from a quarter, you have never visited. In short my escapism had left me stranded, the reverberating church clock of St Sulpice a tintinnabulary reminder of a parting of ways but no recompense for what might have been.

The fact that I have at last been able to face the reality of what actually occurred, so far as it is possible for me to reassemble the pieces of the puzzle, has changed everything. The sadness lingers, the sense of loss, the certain knowledge of the irremediable end of my marriage to the person I loved best. Yet the pain and passion are intertwined; they are now a part of me. And as my awareness of these dual companions of my damaged heart deepens, I find I am learning to accept the whole.

Dutifully, as if out of respect for my changed demands, the blue garden, which for so long helped to lighten the way through the dark of my despair, has receded from my nights, flickering back only once in recent weeks, and then only very briefly, its screen lifting not on to Paris, not on to anywhere I can recollect. In this virtual snapshot, it was so short-lived, I stood by a lake, looking across its still surface. In the foreground was a spread of lilies whose cupped blooms opened in vivid pinks and yellows. I walked upon the surrounding mat of leaves, and then as I reached down to pick one of the blossoms I began to sink. At this I felt no fear but a pleasing, warm sensation along my limbs as I lay back floating in this lush water garden in the way one does in a buoyant sea. When I woke up in the comfort of my bed I had a wonderful sense of well-being, as though I had cast off all my debilities, a feeling that persisted throughout the morning.

3

When my dreams took hold of me my interior world seemed more real than the outside one; I longed for night and tried to shrug off the day. In my waking hours my fellows at the home, with the exception of Trudi, enforced the illusion that I was participating in some sort of charade or soap opera into which I had been coerced. At times they spoke their lines as though they had disinterred them among the banal conundrums unrolled from crackers like those silly paper hats we had donned at Christmas. In recording them I may have had occasional lapses of memory and made minor errors in transcription, it is true, but I have conveyed their essence without fear or favour and as accurately as I can. And then days went by when the verbal exchanges I witnessed at lunchtime and elsewhere were repetitious or had a purely utilitarian function, and sometimes I was too preoccupied with my own thoughts and anxieties to listen to what was being said.

I am a bit fatigued, I must say, by the new main topic of the day: Denbigh's elopement and its possible ramifications. On the matter of motivation and the destination of the unlikely couple we are all groping in the middle mist and have nothing useful to contribute. Not that that has ever stopped anyone from having his or her say about almost anything. Rosie hasn't issued a statement on the affair, or rather *affaire*, but she has let it be known by implication or for example reference to the outside help she has had to enlist that Denbigh is not around any more.

In fact in the privacy of my room she said baldly: 'Did you know Denbigh's done a bunk with a floosie from the pub?' I said I did and was sorry she had been left in the lurch, from the point of view of the nursing home. After her earlier admissions to me about him I couldn't bring myself to commiserate with her beyond that. Anyway, in the long run she may well be better off without him. She didn't elaborate at all and nor did I venture more, but I am glad she has cleared the air so that neither of us need pretend that life is just a bowl of cherries in the Durrances' napery nook.

Before she left my room Rosie told me that she is taking on a new nurse, experienced in looking after the elderly, whom she is sure 'the patients' will like. Jacqueline is to be a replacement for Little Jo, who is getting married and will shortly be going to join her husband, an engineer, in Dubai. Meanwhile the residents and staff are being asked to contribute towards a joint wedding present. Little Jo was very popular and I for one shall be sad to see her go. Saddest of all, I expect, will be Sybil, whose favourite she has been. No doubt Caspar, too, will feel wistful about her departure. His famous escapade in the tub has long been forgotten, and though at the time it provoked some merriment, it was never taken as a serious slur on Little Jo's virginity. I think it must have been Ben who tagged the incident 'Caspar's Last Stand'.

I was seated in a chair in my pyjamas and dressing-gown having a sneezing fit in my room when Alice introduced me to the new nurse. I am prone to hay fever and there must have been some early pollen in the air. So I couldn't take her in properly, and since my back was against the daylight, she couldn't have made much of me either. In the circumstances she and Alice stayed with me only very briefly.

I was mystified when I stopped sneezing a few minutes later by the scent left behind in my room. I couldn't recall Alice wearing it in the past and presumed therefore that it must be what the new nurse used. It was a touch exotic and somehow not quite appropriate for Saxton House. Yet there was something vaguely familiar about it, provocative of old memories, stirring the settled dust like a current of air riffling sachets of pollen that had made me sneeze.

I got up and dressed and stood by the window as I often did in the morning, looking down at the garden. With the sun glowing it was already almost warm enough to sit out in the open. I was still standing there gazing into the middle distance when a while later the door opened and the new nurse entered. She seemed to glide in, softly, stealthily, like a sprite on a moonbeam, and then she stood very still in front of me. For a moment, seconds, we stared at each other quizzically and then in some confusion, as though our eyelids, opening and shutting at random, disunited, had thrown our glances out of sync; and finally in utter astonishment.

'Michel, c'est impossible! Je n'arrive pas à y croire.'

'Céline! Ce n'est pas vrai?!'

'Oui, c'est moi, Céline. Je me suis pas un fantôme. Vraiment.... Mais qu'est-ce que tu fais ici?... Tu es en bonne santé? Hein?'

On cue, before I had a chance to explain anything, reassure her that, though I was not exactly fighting fit, I was well on the way to making a full recovery from my various malfunctions if not actual maladies, I began to sneeze again. I had barely recovered from this second maddening attack than she came and threw her arms round me, her head nestling on my chest in an attitude I once knew so well. Waves of her pervasive scent, which had mystified me earlier, stole up on me again, and the smell of her skin, oleaceous, oriental, invoked in me a surge of tenderness. I held her close, her small body curving naturally

93

into mine as if it belonged there, her silken black hair, cut slightly shorter now than she used to wear it, against my cheek.

'It's been a long time, hasn't it? Well,' I asked gently but chidingly, 'I think you owe me an explanation, don't you? Tell me, why did you run away? *Why?* Did I do something terribly wrong?'

She shook her head vigorously. '*Non, non, non,*' she said protestingly. '*Mon papa* – it was my father, you see, he died suddenly. I was terribly upset, you know, I just caught the next plane straight home to be with my brother and sisters. We needed each other, we are all very close as you know. I'm sorry, Michel, but I just didn't have time to tell you, I was in such a state, and you weren't there when I rushed back to your apartment on my way to the airport. Truly....' She paused for a moment and then she said, by way of a hollow afterthought, like a painter who adds an extra brushstroke to a certain feature of his canvas, unwittingly spoiling the original effect: 'And you know when I think about it I don't believe you were ever really happy with me, I was never good enough for you, was I?... You still loved Arabella.... Poor Arabella. That was terrible for you, I know. Such a tragedy. And you know I sometimes felt like a cheap substitute for the woman you really loved....'

Her voice trailed away and as we disengaged from each other she fastened me with her almond eyes. She looked so sad, so genuinely moved, as she spoke that I almost believed her. She had always been so plausible, Céline, and there was a time when, taking her many confidences at face value, I had accepted pretty well everything she said. I could hardly question the veracity of her father's death, she wouldn't lie to me about that, but I knew very well that she didn't care a rap about Arabella. She had never known her and any suggestion that she had meas-

94

ured herself against her was, if not plainly self-deceit, patently absurd. I had never compared the two of them in my mind, much less insinuated to Céline that I was doing so. It is true that the ghost of Arabella had seemed at times to peer over my shoulder, but this was just a part of the twinge of guilt I suffered when enjoying the emotional and sexual intimacy of another woman comparatively soon after her death, when my conscience told me I should still be mourning her. Perhaps Céline had sensed this, although it had never interrupted, not for an instant, our compulsive and frantic love-making from the very first day we had met.

At this juncture, as I sit pen in hand with my notebook on the table in front of me in a pool of light from my window, I am not sure whether to press on or go back, look over my shoulder in order to recapitulate something of those months Céline and I shared. In the intervening period I have sometimes questioned my role, my weak or indulgent submission to her moods and sudden caprices, and not least her unconscionable flouting of the law, to which, through shielding her, I became irrepressibly an accessary after the fact. Yet these discomforting reflections have been swiftly suffused by more persuasive ones: the aromatic essence of her lissom body, the fleshly delights to which I so readily succumbed, day after day, night after night, setting aglow a spark in me I had imagined forever extinguished by the wash of tears.

4

The creature who suddenly stepped or rather ran into my life with so improbable, so unique a sense of timing almost threw herself at me.

'*Monsieur, monsieur, il faut m'aider – s'il vous plaît, je vous en supplie.*'

She was very small, standing little more than five feet even in her thick-soled white trainers. In a flimsy black and white anorak, which she wore over what appeared to be a sky-blue track suit, she was dripping wet, strands of her long black hair sticking to her cheeks and forehead, partly obscuring her pale face. At first I took her for a child. Perhaps she had become separated from her family; perhaps she was lost; perhaps someone had tried to abduct her. Paris, no less than so many cities, is crowded with desperadoes and hazards. Desperate or damaged or unscrupulous figures lurk among its streets and boulevards, along with terrorists, displaced political activists, murderers and madmen, evil men and women of all shades and races. If the world were an oyster the grit to be found inside it might at times seem disproportionate when set beside the pearls. No doubt this is what religious folk would call God's order of things.

'*Je suis en difficulté ... la police ... je vous en prie, aidez-moi.*'

Just as the girl said this, I heard the manic clarion of what I took to be a police car and already I could see a number of policemen, maybe as many as six, coming into the gardens from the direction of the Palais du Luxembourg. They looked this way and that and then separated into twos and started trotting in different directions. Two of them were heading towards where I was standing with the girl under the trees.

'*Monsieur, monsieur....*'

'All right, *mademoiselle*. All right.'

At this I put my arms round her protectively, reassuringly, and as I did so I bent over her, pressing my face against her hair. A bubble of a strange sweet scent floated up. She clung to me with a piteous urgency and she was trembling hard with all the terror of a cornered animal. Then, reaching inside her anorak, she took out a small flat box of some kind and said, speaking in soft but urgent French, 'Here, take it. Take this. Hide it, *monsieur*.'

She pressed the box into my hand and I put it straight away in the inside pocket of my jacket. As I did so, in one movement I pulled the girl firmly against the stem of a chestnut tree, trying to obscure her as best I could from the nearest pair of policemen. From a distance we could have been taken for lovers in a deep embrace trying to shelter from the sheeting rain. In any event the ruse seemed to work because the policemen stopped and after conferring for a minute or two turned round and started to retreat towards the palace. Probably they had had enough of the rain, and they must have recognised that further pursuit of an unsighted quarry would be a purposeless exercise. When they had dispersed I let go of the girl.

'Have they gone, *monsieur*?'

'Yes. Yes, they've gone.'

'You are sure?'

'I promise you. They are nowhere in sight.'

'Thank you, *monsieur*. Thank you for coming to my rescue.'

'It was you who came to me to be rescued,' I said with a smile.

At which she smiled back, her lips curling upwards, a sweet full smile, though her face still looked almost bloodless.

'May I take you somewhere? Do you live near here?'

'No, no, it's not too far really. I live in Montmartre ... near the Sacré Coeur. But I won't go there now. It is not ... it is not safe yet...'

'It doesn't seem too safe for you here either.... You are in some sort of trouble, *mademoiselle*, I can see. I should like to be able to help if I can. And you are very wet. I mean you're wet through....'

She looked up at me and gave a little laugh. 'And you, too, *monsieur*.'

It was true, we were now both all but soaked to the skin. We could just have taken a dip in the pond. It was then that I made a fateful decision. 'You'd better come back to my apartment and dry off,' I said. 'It's quite near here – on the Rue du Bac. We can take a taxi. There's no point in standing out here in the rain any longer.'

She looked hesitant only momentarily and then she thanked me again for my *bienveillance* and said yes she would like to come with me and get dry and everything.

We were lucky to get a taxi quite soon to the Rue du Bac. There we squelched up the long flight of stairs to my studio apartment, leaving a trail of water behind us like fish escaped from a tank. I had thought for a moment that perhaps I should carry her; she was slight enough.

It was a great relief when at last I shut my front door and could take off my shoes and shed my jacket. Then I took the girl's trainers and led her straight to the bathroom, where I told her she could use my towelled bathrobe when she had washed and dried herself. I say 'bathroom' when it was barely more than a hole-in-the-wall niche, yet it boasted a WC and wash-basin as well as a hip-bath with a shower unit. Next I removed the rest of my wet clothes, dried myself and put on a clean shirt and trousers.

The girl spent an age in the bathroom but at last she emerged, barefooted, with otherwise only her hands and neck and face peeping out of my bathrobe, in which she looked more diminutive than ever, like a little waif. She had combed her hair back so that I could see her face properly for the first time. She had a sallow complexion, cupid lips, shining dark eyes and unmistakably oriental features – Chinese probably, though her nose was more European than typically buttonlike. Her hands, which she revealed by rolling back the sleeves of my bathrobe, were delicate, with long, but not over-long, finger-nails cut square at the tips. They were not polished but well manicured, as were her charming slender feet. I thought she was probably in her twenties, though she could have been even younger.

She had wrung out her clothes in the bathroom and I now brought these into the studio and hung them to dry out on a trestle in front of the radiator by the set of tall windows which looked out across a medley of rooftops. These windows opened out on to a small balcony from where you could see the street four storeys below. I asked her if she was hungry and she said yes, *affamée*, starving, so leaving her curled up snugly on the sofa I went into the kitchen and made sandwiches with cheese and baguettes which I had bought fresh that morning and percolated some coffee. Having completed these preparations I put everything on a tray and carried it into the studio, where I set it down on a low marble-topped table in front of the sofa, along with a bowl of fruit. As I did so the girl gave a yelp of delight. 'Oh how lovely, *monsieur*. This is just what I want,' she said with a wide smile, showing perfect white teeth, her eyes gleaming, and fluttering her

99

hands in an upward movement – as if she might suddenly fly out of my bathrobe and whirr in suspended animation like a humming-bird. She reached towards me as I sat down beside her and pressed my hand with hers, her way of thanking me, I guessed, for the modest snack I was offering her. Her skin was soft and cool to the touch as a dewy petal.

With her smile, and the appreciative gesture that followed it, was it then that a new chapter in my life began? Dismiss if you will as noxious, sentimental mush that business about fate and all the rest of it, but just when one imagines that the drama of love is over and done with, that there can be no recovery for your fragmented heart, there comes back to you a tremor as if from a lost land, mutable but insistent, and you know you are being summoned yet again to fling yourself with rapture upon its preternatural shores.

'My name is Michael,' I said, 'so please call me that or...'

'Michael. That's the English way, of course. I like Michael,' she said reflectively, 'but I prefer Michel, I think – especially *en France, en Paris*. Yes, may I call you Michel, please?'

'Very well. And your name?'

'Jacqueline – well, Céline. I used to be called Jacqueline, my parents called me Jacqueline, but now everyone calls me Céline. I'm Céline Coustain.'

'Céline Coustain.' I looked her straight in the eyes as I repeated her name. 'Céline.... That's pretty. I don't know anyone called Céline...'

'Ah, but you do now,' she said smiling.

We sat back sipping our coffee, savouring its fragrance, enjoying the pleasant warmth of the studio, its snugness emphasised by the rain rattling against the window-panes. I was struck by Céline's ease of manner, a surprising contradistinction beside her deceptively childlike appearance. Yet hers was a more natural quality than a veneer of sophistication; rather it hinted at a womanliness born of experience. Experience of what? How had she lived? Where had she sprung from? What on earth had she become involved in that had set six policemen in pursuit of her? And there was that police car, too, which I had heard in the near-distance when I held her in my arms against the chestnut tree as though in a pre-emptive act of love. Maybe they were still trawling the streets for her, for this naïve-looking girl with the radiant smile and slanting eyes.

When we had drunk our coffee and eaten our sandwiches I got up from the sofa and went over to fetch the box that Céline had urged me to take from her and which I had left in my jacket, now drying on the back of a chair. I felt inside and at first couldn't find it. Then I realised that my wallet pocket was torn and the box had slipped through the rent right down inside the lining – an almost perfect place of concealment where it could easily have stayed hidden for days. I eased it out and held it for a moment. Still damp from the rain, it fitted neatly into the palm of my hand. It was a slim rectangular box of dark-red velvet with a press-button opener, evidently a jewel-case of some kind.

I took it over to Céline. 'Here,' I said. 'Here's the box you gave me in the Jardin du Luxembourg.' Then I waited for the moment of truth.

I waited in vain. Céline merely thanked me and tucked the box into a side pocket of my bathrobe. She took it from me quite matter-of-factly, with no outward sign of unease or embarrassment. As I came to discover, she showed fear but never appeared embarrassed in the conventional sense by anything. I found this an attractive trait, it relieved one of spurious prevarication, of pretence, of

101

the need to say this when you meant that, yet it could also be disconcerting, as for instance when one confronted her over some presumed misdemeanour and she simply laughed it off as if it were of no account whatever. That made me feel puffed up, a self-righteous prig who fancied he occupied the high moral ground, a figure of fun in a satirical cartoon with some sanctimonious absurdity ballooning out of his mouth. Of course Céline was perfectly well aware of the effect she could have on me, how easily she could prick and deflate any show of blimpishness with a little dart of a smile aimed deftly and with precision from the right angle at the right moment, how simple it was for her to deflect criticism with a mere shrug of the shoulders. With these diversionary tricks of expression, performed with guile but with such effortless good timing that they seemed innocently spontaneous, she was to some extent playing on the disparity of our ages. A man past his prime and as infatuated as I became is in certain respects no match for a heedless girl, young enough to be his offspring, who is the object of his amorous compulsion. Céline knew very well that I wished to avoid placing a distance between us by dragging my feet over some apparent inconsistency of behaviour on her part. She was young, impatient to move on, eager to enjoy herself; reprimands were for children, and anyway I was not her keeper. Not yet, anyway.

However, I am jumping events; these insights I was to acquire later on. For the present, at this first tête-à-tête of ours in the Rue du Bac as she sat beside me with a mysterious box in her pocket, an erstwhile fugitive from the police, I thought I deserved to be taken into her confidence.

'Well, Céline,' I began ponderously, like a presiding magistrate in a court of law, 'is there anything you would like to tell me about ... about what happened this morning...?'

'Happened? Oh, *monsieur* – Michel, I mean – *Je ne vois pas à quoi cela peut servir.*'

'What's the problem then?'

'*Pas de problème. Il n'y a pas de problème.*'

'But you wouldn't be here at all if there was no problem, as you say…'

'Yes, but you see there is nothing I can tell you…. There is nothing I feel it is fair to tell you. It is all too *embrouillé*, too complicated. *Vous comprenez? Vous voyez?*'

I tried one more gambit. It was pretty well my last card and, quick-witted as she was, often a mental step ahead of me, Céline must have suspected I would play it.

'The box,' I said. 'What about the box? What's in that box, may I ask, which needed guarding so urgently?'

'It is nothing, Michel…. It is nothing. It is just something I am looking after for a friend…. I didn't want to drop it, you see. I was worried I might drop it somewhere and lose it. Now I can return it to my friend.'

By early evening Céline's track suit and anorak were still too damp for her to put on. Meanwhile I had lent her a shirt and some ankle socks of Arabella's I found in one of my drawers, which she could at least walk around in, her own underclothes having dried off. She looked cute in this outfit, frisking round the studio and wiping her nose on her shirt-sleeves in childlike fashion. We were both hungry, so I made an omelette with a green salad and opened a bottle of wine. It was wonderful to share supper again with a pretty girl and I lit candles on the table where we sat, to complete the intimate picture. A winter moth whirled giddily round them as we lingered there, drawn as irresistibly towards the blue-white flames as my eyes were by my pert companion.

It was past midnight when Céline asked if she could stay

overnight – yes, the sofa would be lovely. She didn't feel inclined to travel back to Montmartre at so late an hour and it would be difficult to find a taxi. So I left her snuggled up under a rug and then lay down on my divan, where I fell into a deep, dreamless sleep.

I don't know whether or not she planned it or if the move was a spontaneous one, it could have been a bit of both, but my next conscious moment came when I felt Céline slide down inside my bed. Then with delicacy and assurance she took me in her mouth. Maybe this was some rite of gratitude from the East where for centuries the phallus was revered, where the God of Egypt spewed out his sperm and made the universe. Yet it would be coy to make excuses for allowing this young girl to awaken me, to arouse me from my deadness with her loving tongue. How urgently did I then kiss her secret places, taste the moist peregrine flesh, her moans of joy confused in the sound of thrashing rain, her hands clawing the sheets, my back, lilies with talons. And as our bodies interlaced, our sexual heat intensified and expanded, and it all began to happen.

5

When I awoke at midday she was gone. I had an instant terrible pang, a feeling of abandonment. And with it came not sadness, sadness is the wrong word, but a sense of loving and losing all over again. A sense not of rejection but of insufficiency, though that doesn't quite explain it either. I suppose it had something to do with the loss of confidence I had suffered through living alone all those lean months since Arabella had died. It wasn't that I thought there could be no other woman in my life; nothing so negative had crystallised in my mind. I just hadn't contemplated anyone else, a substitute I could put in her place, some virescent female shape assuming her selfsame clothes but without identity. Besides, I could hardly fantasise about anyone else, any other woman, while I was still tramping the streets in search of Arabella, imagining I had caught glimpses of her here and there.

Except for the fragrance of her body, a spicy mix perfuming my sheets, there was nothing left of Céline in the studio to suggest she had ever been there. She had even straightened and patted down the cushions on the sofa before she left and neatly folded the rug. The little box? It was no longer in my bathrobe pocket, so she must have taken it. I thought she might at least have left me a note with her telephone number, but no – nothing. I tried the directory: there were a few Coustains but none in Montmartre. I told myself that she would have written down my number. Anyhow she knew where to find me.

105

There was nothing I could do; I had no means of reaching her.

Two days later and I had still had no word from Céline. Meanwhile, when I sat in a bus I noticed an item in a newspaper left behind on the seat. This described briefly an attempted robbery from a jeweller on the Rue de Médicis. The thieves didn't get far with their haul. The triggering of an alarm system by an alert assistant had quickly brought the police, who apprehended two masked men nearby. However, one item which they had dropped in a scuffle in the street was apparently picked up by an accomplice, who ran off with it. This was described as a diamond bracelet valued at 200,000 francs. So far it had not been traced and the police were therefore anxious to question any witnesses to the crime. A substantial reward was being offered for the safe return of the missing jewel.

So that was it; everything fitted. No description was given of the third party but I had little or no doubt on the matter. Céline was a thief. I had befriended a common thief. Befriended was a euphemism. The fact was that, just as she had snatched up the stolen bracelet, I had snatched her from under the noses of the police. Snatched her for myself; taken her to my apartment, dressed and fed her, then undressed and fornicated with her. I thought of her now, the taste of her lips, her fluffy wet orifice, her sweet firm breasts, her erect nipples, her thighs against mine, her legs wrapped round me; and her whimperings of pleasure, her erotic urgings, animal cries. She could have stripped the vaults of the Banque de France of bars of gold for all I cared, I still wanted her back. *Céline, Céline, Céline*. I repeated her name aloud as I climbed the stairs up to my studio. Perhaps she had come back there, pushed a note through the letter-box when she rang my doorbell and there was no reply. No, there was nothing.

She had vanished into thin air as enigmatically as she had materialised out of it. A will-o'-the-wisp.

I poured myself a large cognac and sat down on the sofa, reflecting on what she had told me about herself. Perhaps by means of a simple recitation of the details of her life as I had understood them, accepting them as fact, I might fasten on some clue as to why and when she had resorted to a life of crime, if indeed that were the case. I didn't seriously believe I would detect any such chink of enlightenment but it made me feel near her again, that she actually existed and was not simply a figment of my imagination, a bewitching phantasm I had conjured up in my pilgrimage to the Jardin du Luxembourg.

She was born in Saigon, the youngest daughter (one of six siblings) of a Chinese father and French mother, her parents, both Catholics, having met and married in what had formerly been French Indo-China. Despite the successive war years, her father had prospered as a small trader, especially during the time of the American intervention. After school she had trained as a nurse, but when her mother died she had left Vietnam, that tragic country plundered and mutilated for its own good. First she went to London, where she worked for two years as an au pair with an Italian diplomat and his family. She quitted them when her employer tried one too many times to seduce her and immediately came to Paris, where she had lived ever since.

She had kept her original name, Jacqueline ('Jackie') Chen, in England, but had adopted her own second forename and her mother's maiden name once she had decided to stay on in France. She had learned English at school but French was virtually her first language and she had soon adapted to the French way of life. Finding work had sometimes been a problem. She did a short stint as an auxiliary nurse, but found the hospital regime too dictatorial, even racist she implied, and had subsequently done a variety of jobs – serving in cafés, and working for a short while as a cleaner at the Crillon. Then she had an affair with a Swiss banker, a married man she had first met doing out his room at the hotel, which drifted on until he was posted back to Geneva. That had been a good spell. Her lover, a kindly if prosaic man in his early fifties, was affluent and could afford to spoil her. Latterly, however, her life had been a bit up and down, more down than up it seemed, but she felt at home in Paris and had no plans to move elsewhere.

As she told me all this she didn't strike me as someone who planned things in any detail. It was the place, where she lived, that counted most. What she actually did there seemed a secondary consideration. Probably this lack of purpose derived from the uncertainties overshadowing her early life, in which refugees, transients of all kinds were rife, while her eldest brother was killed in the fighting. As for friends, she struck me as a loner, not as any kind of groupie, despite her reference to 'everyone' calling her Céline. By that I expect she had meant merely those with whom she came into daily contact, occasional colleagues, her current employer and suchlike. Then of course there was the 'friend' for whom she said she was minding the mysterious box. A man with a mask, it transpired, a criminal, one more piece of grit in the pearly oyster. She had been a nurse, an au pair, swept the muck from under the fat cats in the Crillon, screwed one of them, randy André, and now she was trying her hand as a gangster's moll. How successful she was in that role still seemed open to question, to say the least. But for me, the last lucky link in the chain, a kind of honorary member of the gang, albeit a vital aide, she too would now probably be behind bars.

I began pacing the studio, stopping every so often to refill my glass with cognac. I was slowly getting drunk and felt my cheeks flushing from the alcohol, the walls of the studio gradually closing in on me. I felt trapped; I needed fresh air.

It was a relief to get out and I walked purposefully across the boulevard, my destination the Rue de Médicis. Once there I soon located the jeweller where the attempted robbery had taken place, the only possible one in the vicinity. Outside stood a solitary policeman, as if on sentry duty, speaking into a walkie-talkie. He eyed me quizzically when I went up to look in the window, itself undamaged, but there was no visible sign that anything untoward had occurred. It was a good-class shop and in fact there were only a few select items on display. I didn't linger there and was inevitably drawn across the street to the Jardin du Luxembourg. I went right up to the tree where I had held Céline willingly captive, secure from her pursuers, paused there for a minute or two as if to assure myself of its actuality, then wended my way back to my apartment via the market stalls on the Rue de Seine, where I bought some groceries and a bottle of cognac.

This little expedition hardly alleviated my feeling of restlessness but it helped clear my head, and it confirmed 'beyond reasonable doubt', as they say, my suspicions of Céline's involvement in the theft of the bracelet, though as I reminded myself I hadn't actually opened the box she had entrusted to me, nor had I looked inside it for the incriminating evidence. It is not my way. I am not given to nosing in people's handbags, exploring their furniture, reading their personal postcards. Yet in Céline's case I wished I had done so. I could then have confronted her, got to the root of the matter, even – heaven knows – persuaded her to return the stolen piece. Now it was too late and all I could do was to sit and wait in the hope that sooner or later she would contact me. She sat perched on my mind like a fallen angel.

6

Before I met Arabella it was not exceptional for me to sleep casually with a girl and then forget all about her. This was the norm for young men and women in the cosmopolitan and Bohemian circles in which I mixed. However, I was in a very different situation now, much older as I was and living alone in a foreign city without any friends. I had of course deliberately chosen my solitude; for me it was perhaps a necessary form of emotional convalescence to withdraw from all but cursory social contact with anyone. Nevertheless, as was evidenced later on by the nightly vigils I was to keep in my blue garden, I never fully entered or accepted a state of bereavement. Instead I constructed a zone of make-believe and wish-fulfilment in my mind in which I could continue to exist without wrenching myself irrevocably from the past. I was quite unaware that this private zone was vulnerable to intrusion by another from the outside and ill prepared for the effect that that eventuality might have on me. I had spent a single night with a girl I had never met before and yet it was as if she had always been there waiting in the wings to enter my life. And because of the intuitive way she had flown towards me, drawn into my aura as it were by a cosmic beam, I could not accept that she had fluttered out of it as though I were a mere resting-place for a bird of passage.

*   *   *

Two weeks went by and there was still no sign of Céline. I knew so little about her, practically nothing of her daily habits and movements, and so I could hazard only wild guesses as to what had become of her. Maybe she had been trying to dispose of the stolen bracelet, and if she had been successful in selling it, had pocketed the entire proceeds. If there were other members of the gang they would be as anxious to catch up with her as the police, in which case she might have run to ground or left the city altogether.

Mystified and frustrated I decided to take an exploratory trip to Montmartre, where Céline had told me she lived. I took the Métro to Château Rouge and walked from there to the Sacré Coeur, the only direction finder she had given me. It was a bitter morning, the freeze unalleviated by a wan sun, and there were still patches of ice on the pavements. I walked warily round the deserted streets, diving into a couple of cafés to warm up, and then had an early snack lunch. I became so cold when I emerged outside afterwards that on a sudden whim I went into a cinema. I had already seen one of the movies, I didn't fancy a spaghetti Western, so settled for the third option. As I should have realised if I had paid proper attention to the billboard outside, this turned out to be a blue movie. There was only a thin scattering of people in the auditorium, a few single men hunched in their seats and two rows behind me a young couple who, I surmised, as the antics on the screen became more lurid, began stimulating each other, sighing and giggling as they did so. In front it was all organs and orgasms but no true passion, the sexual athletics unredeemed by a dreadful dubbed French script, adapted presumably from the original moronic Scandinavian. But the warmth of the cinema was comforting, and before long this and the sheer monotony of the multiple couplings had a soporific effect on me.

111

Consequently I found myself being nudged by the female attendant, who said sharply in an undertone that I must stop snoring or vacate my seat forthwith. I had been creating a disturbance.

I got up and started to grope my way along the seats towards the exit. As I passed by their row the amorous couple, whose scarcely disguised titillations I had heard, disengaged from each other and made snorting noises at me, sniggering lewdly. You could hardly blame them; it was that sort of place.

A blankness followed, during which I lost count of the days. They merged greyly without anything happening to distinguish one from the other. It was partly because of the bleak weather, which discouraged me from going out of doors except with the object of replenishing my larder with the bare essentials, bread and milk and so forth. I was drinking too much and eating too little as inertia gripped me in a strangle-hold. At night I slept fitfully. Yet again there were times when I fancied Céline was purely a dream-figure who had become confused in my mind with Arabella while I had sought to fill the void of her absence. Although on the one hand I had refused all along to accept that Arabella had died, on the other I was now trying to deny that Céline could ever have existed. In moments of lucidity, when I was more or less sober, I realised it was my re-experiencing of companionship as much as intense sexual pleasure in the hours I had shared with Céline, joy given and then withdrawn, that was uptilting my sense of balance. Once, and only once, the telephone rang, jangling my nerve-ends, but the caller had the wrong number.

Several weeks, perhaps a whole month, I forget now, went by before Céline came back into my life. I had traipsed round the permanent art exhibition at the

112

Beaubourg. It was a Saturday and so I went there early before the usual hordes descended on the place. I was in a distracted frame of mind and I gave the pictures only cursory attention. Afterwards, as I sat in the cafeteria, she suddenly alighted by my side like one of those pigeons that swoop down from the rafters for bits of food dropped by nibblers from the tables.

'Michel! Enfin je t'ai retrouvé! C'est merveilleux. C'est étonnant.'

'You!' I said flatly, then with some fervour, aggrieved: 'You never rang me.... You knew my number?'

At this she threw her arms round me and I held her tight, smelling her curious aromatic odour. I kissed her neck, then pressed her lips with mine. We sat down at the table, holding hands like a courting couple and searching each other's eyes. She looked wonderfully pretty in a black turtle-neck sweater and charcoal-grey skirt, the first time I had ever seen her dressed properly.

She smiled her electric smile. 'Mon bien-aimé, I did take your phone number, honestly, but stupidly I lost it. I was so upset, I can't tell you. I know where you live, on the Rue du Bac of course, but I couldn't remember the number and.... You see, we arrived there in the pouring rain and I didn't take anything in properly then. And you never told me your surname, so I couldn't look you up in the directory, even if you are listed. I don't know what to say except how sorry I am and how much I've missed you. Oh, I've missed you so much...'

'I've missed you too.'

'You know, I've come here several times to look for you, mon bien-aimé, please believe me, because you told me it was one of your favourite places, but you never showed up until now.... You look tired. What have you been doing to yourself? You haven't been looking after yourself, have you? You are quite ... grey.'

113

'You mean my hair has changed colour?' I quipped drily. I wanted to tell her then and there how dreadfully, frantically I had missed her, how wretched I had been all these dreary days, that I would never let go of her again, but I held back out of fear that if I pressed too hard I might frighten her off. I knew enough about women and of love to be aware that you must always hold something in reserve, that you can't imprison a woman, shut her in a box like a caterpillar with holes for air. You must bide your time, be tremendously patient – the truisms slide easily enough off the tongue but are less easy to heed. I have learned the lessons of love the hard way, but I am too impulsive to be crafty, to lie in wait for the object of my desire like a fox. I was aware, too, as I sat beside her looking down upon the wide montage of rooftops, pigeons scavenging at our feet, that Céline was less than half my age, that my ageing heart was like a tinder-box, ever vulnerable to a flash of her smile.

Of course I didn't sit there in the cafeteria deliberating prosaically, calculating, weighing pros and cons. I was completely taken up with relief and delight at being with Céline again; my anxieties fled. She was so engaging to be with, so easy to talk to. Her presence both enraptured and soothed me. If I was hesitant in declaring my love for her, it was essentially instinct, hidden strains of self-preservation to which I clung, that held me in check.

We sat on in the cafeteria and had a salad lunch, washed down with glasses of red wine and Badoit. The whole time we managed not to mention the odd circumstances that had brought us together, when Céline had sprinted towards me through the pelting rain like a frightened doe. In my spasmodic reading of newspapers, I had seen no further reference to the failed robbery on the Rue de Médicis, and again intuition told me not to question Céline about it. If she had anything further to say on the subject, she would tell me in her own good time. I still felt uneasy about the whole affair, that Céline had a murky secret from which for all her apparent openness and winsome spontaneity she was deliberately excluding me.

I took her back to my apartment, where we made love with the same ardour as on our first night together. She said she was so happy with me, wouldn't it be wonderful if we could be together all the time – well, you know, at night and everything? I said well, why not, it could be arranged, knowing no arrangements were necessary. As far as I was concerned, she could move in with me straight away. But I didn't tell her this there and then, I didn't spell it out. There was no need, after all. She knew perfectly well how available I was; she knew pretty well the aimless sort of life I was living. Perhaps this was the problem: I was just a bit too available, too easily at her disposal. And in the absence of any regular occupation for either of us, what would we do all day? When we made love we almost sucked our passion dry, and we couldn't do that all day long, even in a honeymoon period, or certainly I couldn't.

I asked her tentatively, affecting off-handedness, if she was doing anything now, during weekdays, meaning some kind of work, and she said no, she was doing nothing at the moment. I didn't take this to imply she was actually looking around for something to do during a temporary lull, but rather that she had shelved things for the time being. I was puzzled how she managed to live meanwhile, how she could afford daily essentials, food and suchlike, without some sort of income, but I stopped myself from asking the obvious question. As I had discovered, she had her own way of dodging or deflecting questions she didn't wish to answer. She was adept at this, like a politician, breezily nonchalant about it. She said whatever came into her head, it didn't matter what so long as it got

115

her off the hook. Next question, please. Or don't bother, *monsieur*, Michel, *mon chéri, mon bien-aimé*. It was a game to her. She was as perceptive as she was sharp-witted; she knew all along when I knew that she knew the simple answer to a simple question. It just amazed me how she could make her often blatant inconsistencies sound quite rational.

So did she really want to come and live with me? It was evening, we had had our supper and were sitting on the sofa drinking coffee. I wasn't asking her to commit herself indefinitely, suggesting we should draw up some sort of unofficial contract, but there it was, I would gladly have her here if she felt so inclined. I came out with this straight, like that.

That would be really lovely, she said, but to begin with could she come at weekends, say on Friday evening and stay over till Monday morning perhaps? We could go to galleries and concerts and everything, and that would be really nice.

I thought that was smart thinking on her part and actually the best arrangement, from the short-term point of view anyway. We wouldn't be in each other's company long enough to feel trapped by it, and there would always be something to look forward to. The blankness would go out of my life.

She asked if she could maybe bring round some of her clothes and leave them with me, if there was room you know, so she wouldn't have to pack a bag each week. It would simplify things for her – and my bathrobe was far too big for her to change into anyway, she added, smiling her adorable smile. That did sound like a commitment, that she meant what she said. I felt thrilled, almost ecstatic.

116

The following afternoon, Sunday, we went to Montmartre to collect Céline's clothes from the Rue de Bonne. She lived in a dilapitated-looking house where she had a tiny room which you reached by climbing a narrow, dingy iron staircase. However, the living-room itself, a bed-sitter with somewhat primitive cooking facilities, was newly painted and attractively furnished. The walls were primrose yellow, the woodwork white, and she had some charming Chinese paintings on silk in green bamboo frames on display, which had belonged to her mother, she told me. On one side of the room there was a huge television set, far too big for the available space, almost big enough for Céline to jump inside it and gesticulate through the screen. Everything was arranged very tidily, which I thought augured well for her future visits to my apartment, and there was a pleasant after-smell from joss-sticks hanging in the air. I was quite taken aback when she opened her built-in clothes cupboard, which extended almost the length of one wall, by the sheer quantity of clothes squeezed into it. There appeared to be something for every occasion and the dresses and suits looked well laundered, immaculate in fact. Beneath them were rows and rows of shoes lined up with parade-ground precision. I had brought along a brand-new suitcase of Arabella's, never used, in which Céline packed a selection of clothes and shoes, carefully wrapping the latter in tissue paper. Did I have room for all this? she wondered. Good, that was *merveilleux*.

As I stood waiting for her I noticed beside her hair-brushes and comb placed on a small chest of drawers with a looking-glass on top, which evidently Céline used as a dressing-table, the red jewel-case she had thrust into my hand at our first encounter. She had eyes as keen as a cat's and saw me notice it at a glance.

'Ah, Michel, you are wondering about my little box, *hein*? Well, let me tell you something, *chéri*. When I came

117

back here and opened it up – I hadn't looked before, you know – *zut alors*, it was empty! There was nothing inside, absolutely nothing! Whatever was inside must have fallen out, you know, maybe in the *jardin*. I don't know. I just don't know. Anyway my friend said it didn't matter, she was going to sell it and it was insured. Well now, wasn't that *extraordinaire*? Unfortunately the box got stained, from the wet, so my friend said it was no good to her any more and so I have kept it for some of *my* little things.' At which she went over and opened the jewel-case, which had been the property of a 'friend', a woman apparently, not part of the swag dropped by a bandit on the run, a man with a mask.

It was true, the burgundy silk lining inside the lid of the jewel-case was discoloured, the velvet cushioning soiled. It held a few small pieces of jewellery, drop earrings, a diamanté brooch, a silver pin with a pearl, that sort of thing. Céline clipped it shut and then put it, with a single hairbrush and comb, alongside the rest of her belongings in the suitcase. 'I'll take it with me,' she said. 'That'll be nice. Now you don't need to worry about it any more, *mon chéri*, do you? *Pas de problème, hein?*'

Well, that was that, then. So far as Céline was concerned, that was the end of the matter. The jewel-case had been empty all along, you see. Joke over. No problem.

7

Céline liked things to be nice, just so, and she arranged her belongings discreetly in my apartment such that you would hardly have known she was there. She was tactful and unobtrusive and deferred to me with what I suppose was an oriental approach to a man. But I didn't see her as a slave-girl or plaything. I tried to make her understand from the outset that what would give me the greatest pleasure was the feeling that we could share things. I loved to see her happy, laughing; and for me her effervescence, her sheer zest for life, was inspirational, a tonic. For months I had closed in on myself, everything was an effort, everything dragged; I couldn't look ahead. With Céline I was invigorated, young again, there was nothing I felt I couldn't do.

We did all sorts of things, from looking at pictures to dancing in jazz clubs, and then we took trips outside the city – to Versailles and Fontainebleau and Malmaison (where, apparently out of snobbery towards the tourist circuit, Céline's banker friend André hadn't deigned to set foot) – picknicking when spring came, encrusting the ground with flowers. We'd take a train to the country and get off when we liked the look of somewhere, walk around, lie under the burgeoning trees where we fondled each other and kissed. Sometimes we became aroused to such a pitch that we felt impelled to hasten back to the studio and make love. 'Let's make babies,' Céline would whisper playfully. 'Oh please, Michel, give me a baby.'

Hardly code words that needed cracking. However, I refused to make love in the open as Céline would have liked. I was too old for that.

She was not naïve, her femininity was mature, yet she had an enchanting air of innocence, took such palpable delight in small pleasures, arranging the table for supper with special touches, spring flowers cut just so, wineglasses sparkling, napkins freshly pressed, one day shaped into fans, the next into mitres, or lilies, fleurs-de-lis. With her touch simple meals became little festivals, piquant, succulent, each in its turn to be savoured, relished. We prepared food together and took it in turns to do the cooking, and Céline introduced me to various Vietnamese dishes as well as making more familiar Chinese ones. And occasionally we dined at a Vietnamese restaurant in the Quartier Latin, Céline giving me expert guidance on the menu. She brought the studio alive with plants and cut flowers and bowls of fruit, rearranging a few ornaments I had collected during my time in Paris and unearthing others that belonged to the owner of the apartment from cupboards. And she persuaded me to buy some scatter cushions and a raw silk throw, which we arranged on the sofa and chairs, and some mock-sheepskin rugs. With these artefacts the rather drab look of the place was transformed into a quite exotic *ambience*. In the afternoons we would sometimes make love on the large sofa, Céline gently persuading me for her final climax on to one of the soft new rugs beside it. She must have chosen them as much for this purpose as for their decorative aspect.

I was pleased with the new look Céline created in the studio, but she had to use all her powers of persuasion to induce me to buy a television set, the programmes on offer being for the most part abysmal. However, Céline had another motive. This was to indulge her passion for old Hollywood movies, a taste she had acquired strangely enough in Saigon, in whose fleapits she told me they used to be shown. Her male movie heroes were among bygone stars – Gary Cooper, Ronald Colman, Herbert Marshall, Errol Flynn, Franchot Tone – a whole host of them. So I also had to buy a video recorder and a selection of cassettes, of mostly black-and-white movies. She was wildly excited making her choice of these, like a child let loose in a toyshop. Subsequently we spent hours watching them, and sometimes I had difficulty persuading her not to rerun the same movie twice in a row, like a continuous performance in a cinema. She loved identifying people at random, passers-by, women and men in shops and restaurants and so on, with vintage Hollywood stars. 'Look, that woman is just like Claudette Colbert, isn't she?' Or 'Did you see the man over there? He could be Clark Gable.' She said I reminded her of Leslie Howard in *The Scarlet Pimpernel*, oh yes, and my voice too, never mind that Howard was rather younger in his heyday. 'That doesn't matter, *mon chéri*, that's not the point. You have the same *qualité*, the same *essence*.' And whom did her banker friend André resemble? I wondered. Charles Boyer, of course, he was his double.

Once, lunching in La Coupole, we sat near the real Stewart Granger and for one ghastly moment I thought Céline might feel urged to go up to his table and ask for his autograph. But no, she was too sophisticated for that, and anyhow she said she had never cared for him, not at all, she thought he was vulgar, too pleased with himself. I was quite relieved, especially since I had noticed Granger eyeing Céline and, if she had responded, I fancied that the Scarlet Pimpernel could have been provoked into a duel for her favours with the master swashbuckler, of the chandelier-swinging variety. My twinge of jealousy, which I later confessed to Céline, became an ongoing joke between us, and it was that incident in La Coupole which inspired her to give me the endearing sobriquet *ma pimprenelle*, or sometimes 'my pimpernel', depending on her mood of the moment. She interchanged French and English with easy fluency, even when making love.

The ritual, or rather idyll, of our long weekends together in the Rue du Bac continued for several months, interrupted only once when Céline went to stay for a few days with a girl-friend of hers in Rouen, or so she said. I had come to accept, more or less, the fact that Céline, though disarmingly frank in many respects, told me only what she wanted to tell me. I knew when not to press her; there were certain signs. She had a way of pursing her lips, simultaneously averting her gaze or, if she were seated, looking into her lap. These mannerisms were so fleeting, so subtle, it was a while before I was able to interpret the signal they gave out. It was not that I distrusted her, I didn't suspect her of taking another lover, but just supposing for instance André suddenly reappeared, would she not be curious to see him again, even oblige him with a night of love? I couldn't blame her if she did so. She was not exclusively mine; I didn't own her. And besides these were yet early days in our liaison when our passion for each other was fresh, so I had no urge to torment myself with doubt, with thoughts of Céline's possible infidelity. I had confidence in her, and in myself in relation to her. Nevertheless the situation in which we had first met still occupied a corner of my mind, as did the tell-tale red jewel-case a corner of the studio, set on a table with other personal items belonging to Céline.

It was early one evening in midsummer when the episode in the Jardin du Luxembourg was brought back dramatically into focus. Céline and I were idly watching a television news bulletin when an announcement was made that a convicted criminal had escaped while he was being transferred from one prison to another. A still police photograph of the man, full face and profile, flashed on the screen, revealed that he was one of a gang who, among other misdeeds, had tried to rob a jeweller on the Rue de Médicis late in the previous year.

I think I let slip some comment like 'Fancy that' in a rather supercilious undertone, but Céline kept her lips firmly sealed. She seemed indifferent. However, when the young robber's face appeared in front of us, I thought I detected that little trick of hers, almost like a tremor: in a twinkling she glanced down at her lap.

On the Tuesday following, the day after she returned to Montmartre, Céline telephoned me to say that the weather was so nice she had decided to spend a week or so with her friend in Rouen. 'You know, *chéri*, the girl I stayed with last time. You don't mind, do you?' Meanwhile she said she'd like to come and collect a few of her things from the Rue du Bac. It was all right, she wouldn't need to bother me or anything, she'd let herself in and bring her own suitcase – a light one as she wouldn't be gone for long.

I was out when the same day Céline came round to my apartment. When I returned there I saw that she had removed all her personal effects, which she usually kept on a corner table, including the jewel-case. I opened the wardrobe. It was virtually empty of her clothes but for a couple of sarongs which I recalled she had occasionally worn around the studio. I didn't attach much importance to any of this; Céline had her own way of doing things and her last trip to Rouen had barely ruffled our customary routine.

This time in Céline's absence I decided to make a long-delayed visit to Pip and Daphne in London. I had missed seeing them and it was already more than a year since Pip had stayed with me on his way to Reims. Daphne assured me when I rang that they would love to have me for as long as I wanted to stay, and that the children would be thrilled to see me.

In those days they had an attractive terrace house with a small back garden in Notting Hill Gate, not far from Holland Park, and I spent about ten pleasant days with them, playing with the children in the park and reading them endless stories. It was the greatest fun to be with them again. They were at an age of boundless receptivity when interest can be won without undue persuasion and pleasures need not be hunted but come running to your door. For them, to be alive was an adventure in which, as they revelled in their springy limbs beside me, tumbling and cartwheeling like midget circus clowns, they were eager that I too should joyfully participate. I was in two minds as to whether to tell Pip and Daphne about Céline. For one thing, Pip has a puritanical streak in him and the idea of my having a girl younger than he as a lover might I thought earn his disapproval, which would be tiresome and even threaten to throw our own relationship off-balance. But he took it well and said, putting his arm round my shoulder: 'It's your life, Dad, and you must do with it what you think is best for you. I just hope she'll make you happy.'

8

I hadn't deluded myself while I was with Céline that I had attained a state of untrammelled happiness, any more than I believed I had finally despatched sorrow and its miserable attendants. Happiness, as I knew full well, is ephemeral. Scarcely have you imagined you have caught hold of it than it escapes like a butterfly from your hand, zigzagging capriciously out of reach. Yet Céline brought me a new sense of tranquillity, a certain peace of mind. She had her moods, true, linked sometimes to her menstrual periods, and she was given to childish sulking when she thought she might not get her own way, say over how we should spend an afternoon, even about the colour of a cushion. At such moments I usually took the least line of resistance and agreed to her choice or preference. From time to time we bickered – about whose turn it was to prepare the next meal, each stupidly claiming it was ours, that sort of thing – but we never quarrelled hammer and tongs as lovers are supposed to do now and again for their own good. None the less, as though recognising that such natural discord was only to be expected, if not obligatory, and therefore that she should at least pay lip-service to it, Céline would sometimes preface what she was about to tell me with phrases like 'Please don't be angry with me...', or 'I know you'll be cross, *ma pimprenelle*, but...', knowing all the while that her imminent revelation, as likely as not inconsequential, would provoke no ire from me whatever.

125

Of course Céline may have acquired the formula (and – who knows? – with good reason) when she was with André or some other admirer whose identity she hadn't disclosed. For all I knew, André might still be chewing bones of contention on her account, but this could be no more than conjecture on my part and was an avenue down which I had no wish to be diverted. I had never questioned Céline about that part of her life, I simply accepted what she chose to divulge, and as long as we were together I was wholly committed to and preoccupied with the present. If at any time I glanced backwards it was simply to confirm the shifting perspective, the new angles of perception from which I persuaded myself I should now view the past. In short, I should accept that that part of myself I had given Arabella had died with her. That this was not so, that I was soon to be denied any such comfortable illusions, the succeeding course of events was inexorably to reveal.

There was no sign of Céline when I got back to my apartment, and it was quite clear that she hadn't been there in my absence. As I said, she was very neat in her habits, but that didn't mean she could make herself invisible. If she had been around, I should quickly be able to tell. For one thing, I had left a note for her saying where I had gone and giving my London telephone number. It remained untouched where I had placed it on the table in front of the sofa. Moreover she would have made a point of watering the plants (*mes enfants*, she called them), especially as they dried out quickly in the summer; and then there was only the barest whiff in the studio of her unmistakable scent. Of her clothes, there were still just the two sarongs left in the wardrobe, tokens of sensual evenings.

I had returned to Paris on a Thursday, in the hope that

Céline would arrive the following evening. It was not to be. She neither turned up nor telephoned me over the weekend. She could of course have been trying to reach me while I was still in London. I had no means of knowing. She had no telephone herself in her apartment, so I had always had to rely on her contacting me in case of any change of plan.

A week went by and my telephone rang only once. It was Pip, asking if all was well. I didn't tell him about Céline, whose absence was now causing me some anxiety. I recalled the time she had disappeared before, the day after we had first met, but the circumstances had been rather different then. We hadn't set up home together; we owed each other no allegiance. Again, the peculiar business concerning the jewel-case came throbbing back into my mind. What had actually occurred remained a mystery which Céline had made no effort to explain. In fact she had been consistently evasive about it. And then there was that shifty look of hers I had noticed when the pictures of the escaped robber appeared on television. It all seemed to add up, to point in a direction, but to what and where I could make but wild guesses. If only she had confided in me I could have tried to help her, no matter her predicament. It was this secretive silence which I found so frustrating. I couldn't shake off the feeling that something sinister lay behind it.

By now alarmed, I took a taxi to Montmartre. At the Rue de Bonne I mounted the stairs as fast as I could to Céline's apartment. There was an unpleasant smell on the landing outside, a mix of garlic and stale cigarette-smoke and general grunge. I was winded and paused for a moment, then I knocked on Céline's door, its stripped woodwork cracking in places, hoping Céline would look through the spyhole and then let me in. No reply. Next I tried to peer through the keyhole, but the curtain must

127

have been half drawn, for I could barely see a thing inside. The door of the apartment opposite opened a chink, the person within eyeing me suspiciously. '*Madame – pardon, monsieur – est-ce que Mademoiselle Coustain s'en va?*' I asked speciously of the wild-haired young man standing in his doorway, looking me up and down. He shrugged and said he hadn't seen the Chinese lady around recently, suggesting gruffly that I ask the *concierge*. She might know.

I went downstairs to see the *concierge*, a sour-faced, full-bosomed woman in her fifties dressed in the long black habit of another era, her grey hair drawn back and held in place by a pink plastic comb. I explained that I was a friend of Mlle Coustain but could not get any reply when I knocked on her door. Did *Madame* happen to know if she was out of town?

'*Mademoiselle Coustain? Elle est partie.*' The woman went on to say that Mlle Coustain had left the house about three weeks ago. '*Attendez, monsieur,*' she grunted through yellow teeth, shuffling over to a bureau and then consulting what proved to be some sort of rent-book, with ruled columns and headed by numbers, presumably those of rooms in the house. '*Ici,*' she said, pointing with a stubby finger at a page on which Céline's surname was written in ink and beside it a sum of francs, the rent she must have paid. Apparently Mlle Coustain had said she was leaving Paris. At any rate she had vacated her apartment for good, taking all her possessions with her, except for the television set which had been taken away independently – by a purchaser or hire firm perhaps, the *concierge* suggested. The date of her departure, confirmed in the rent-book the *concierge* had shown me, was I realised the same Tuesday Céline had come to pack up her things in the Rue du Bac.

*   *   *

128

When I looked back I sometimes thought how odd it was that, despite fretting for a while, I was able to readjust with relative ease to my former state of solitude. I had become infatuated with Céline, there was no doubt of that. She was habit-forming; when she was around she was as addictive as an aphrodisiac. Yet while the deprivation of certain drugs induces acute withdrawal stresses, my yearning for Céline diminished with her inaccessibility. I suppose it was a case of love without nourishment withering on the vine, curling up and drying out like the plants Céline had left behind in my studio which I neglected watering and eventually had to throw out. I was the poorer without her, and wherever she was she would probably have said the same of me, and who could have anticipated that there were forces waiting to grab hold of her and pull her away? We had come together in a moment of mutual need and I could truthfully say that I was thankful for my good fortune while it had lasted. Now I should try to pick up the pieces of my life and move on.

And move on I had to. In three months the tenancy of my apartment on the Rue du Bac expired. I had an option to renew it but decided not to do so and return instead to England. If Céline had still been there things would no doubt have been different, but there was no longer anything to keep me in Paris. Earlier I had travailed in search of Arabella, and now it was her loss that once again began to take hold of me. It was a cycle of pain from which, before I reached the point of shutting out consciousness to stand on the threshold of my blue garden, with its magnetic lure of rediscovery and revival, I wondered if I could ever break free.

It was when I was packing up the day before my departure from the Rue du Bac that a vital piece of the jigsaw accidentally slid into my hand, both clarifying and confusing what had gone before. I had taken my jacket from the wardrobe and started to fold it to put in a suitcase. As I did so I felt an object in a side pocket, or so I thought, and I put my hand inside to remove it. There was nothing there, and then I realised that whatever it was must be inside the lining. At once I remembered that that was where the jewel-case had lodged, having slipped through a hole, weeks and weeks ago, after the incident in the Jardin du Luxembourg, since when I couldn't recall having worn the jacket. Fearing the worst I held the jacket upside-down and eased my fingers inside the lining. The bracelet which slipped out was composed of three narrow strands of diamonds, with a sapphire clasp at the back. It was delicate and beautiful and even by daylight it came alive in an iridescent cascade.

So what should I do now? I pondered over the alternatives. The insurance money would have long since been paid out to the rightful owner who, I had little doubt, was the jeweller on the Rue de Médicis. A reward had been offered for its return, I recalled from the news item I had read, but I was in no mind to apply for that. Céline had gone, so I couldn't question her, cock my ear for the inevitable evasions.

It didn't take long for me to decide what to do. I went out and bought a small padded envelope, a mini jiffy-bag, and put the bracelet inside, securing the flap with tape. Then I walked to the Rue de Médicis. Where the jeweller's had been, and through whose letter-box I had planned to push the envelope with the bracelet, it was all boarded up. There was no sign outside giving a change of address so I went to enquire at the shop next door. No, they said, the jeweller hadn't moved his business to another address but had closed down altogether – when was it? – three or four months ago, not very long after an awful robbery which had shaken him up badly. Nothing like that had ever occurred in this respectable street before. A widower, he had retired and, so far as they knew, had gone to live in Lyon – or was it Amiens? They really couldn't say. No, he had left no forwarding address. Was I a friend, an old client of his? They gave me his name and said maybe I could try to contact him via the post office or possibly the police.

That night I took the bracelet to the Pont des Arts and flung it into the river. The Seine, witness to a myriad trysts and treacheries, silvered reflector of galaxies, whose plaintive waters had absorbed the drifting white petals of Arabella's body, could keep its crass secret.

9

I am discomfited by Céline's presence at Saxton House.
So far as I am concerned she is in the wrong place at
the wrong time. I was astonished when she spirited herself into my room and I was moved when she embraced
me, but whatever she may think or suppose, it isn't a
matter now of taking up again where we left off. I adjusted
well enough to her disappearance in Paris and I haven't
been pining for her since my return to England. The
simple fact is that during the intervening period, it must
be almost two years, my feelings towards her have cooled.
And I distrust her. I am in no mind to listen to her explanations and excuses any more. I don't want to hear
them; I just don't want to know. I wish I could feel more
kindly disposed towards her, respond to her daily over-
tures of friendliness, for instance to her invitations to
share in her recollections of some of the pleasurable times
we spent together, in themselves harmless enough. 'Do
you remember, *mon chéri*,' she asks with her beguiling
smile, 'that day we were lunching at La Coupole and
Stewart Granger sat near us?' I nod and produce a weak
smile in response so as to make it plain that I wish to
leave it at that. Then she tries another tack, this time with
physical insinuations: 'Oh how I loved those train rides.
You know, when we got out *comme ça* on the spur of the
moment and went for a picnic...', well aware that these
excursions involved as much necking as picnicking. Then:
'Perhaps one afternoon we could go for a picnic some-

where nice near here?' Again I smile my feeble smile but say nothing.

Céline doesn't give up easily. Each day she must hope she'll find a chink in my armour, a way of piercing my defences. She seems unable to get it into her head that all is over between us. I am not trying to punish her, I don't seek revenge, but nor do I wish to play games any more. I've had enough of hide-and-seek, for which of course Céline has shown that she has a special aptitude. I have to think up new ways of keeping her at bay if not quite at arm's distance. For example these days I find that, when I choose, the crusty old semi-invalid façade comes to me all too easily. Then perhaps it isn't a façade: I have become what I appear to be, slotting in out of habit to some preconceptual image, like in reverse an identikit man springing out of a poster and assuming the flesh and blood of the one he represents. It says something for her percipience that Céline can see through my carapace and still reach the soft parts within. With her intimate knowledge of my reflexes gleaned over many months, of the sort only a wife or mistress can gain of a man, she must sense that for all my posturing, my play-acting indifference towards her, my hauteur, in unguarded moments I still lust after her. And she plays on this with an insouciant air. 'Let me help you in the bath, *chéri*,' she said the other day, moistening her cherubic lips with the tip of her pink tongue. 'It must be so difficult for you with your back, *hein*?' 'No, I'm quite all right,' I said brusquely, ungraciously, mindful of Caspar's aborted frolic with Little Jo. What I mean to convey to Céline is that my chandelier-swinging days may be over but I am still quite capable of washing behind my ears unaided. Céline is well aware of this; she was merely testing the ground, giving me a little erotic signal with her tongue. In the evening when she is duty nurse she comes and sits beside me on

133

my bed, stroking my forehead with her cool petal fingers, her coquetry undisguised. With such gestures she plays all the while the considerate, obliging little wife who has always been around, soothing my brow, smoothing my sheets, ready to hold my hand, fasten a loose button with needle and thread. For two pins she would fellate me, no trouble at all, but I am determined to resist seduction, keep my cloistered life intact, remaining monosyllabic in my responses to her various approaches, ever ready to deflect her with a maddening flaccid smile, never mind the nagging state of my member under the bedclothes.

My irritation is ill concealed, too, when she picks up one of my books and starts flicking through the pages with a frown of simulated concentration. I know from our life together in Paris that she is not focused on literature. Sometimes when she was sitting beside me on the sofa or lay curled like a contented puppy on one of the mock-sheepskin rugs at my feet, I would read her a random passage or two that had arrested me in a book, occasionally a poem, but nothing too demanding of her limited concentration, nothing too long, else she would get up in the middle and start moving around the studio, sighing her small sighs and saying vaguely how beautiful that was, patting a cushion, fidgeting with the flowers like a restless toddler seeking yet another distraction.

Fortunately from my point of view the time Céline can spend in my room is restricted by her duties elsewhere, notably the demands of the other residents. Early on she agreed it would be best if we kept the fact that we already knew each other to ourselves, as otherwise our relationship could become the subject of needless speculation which would make life intolerable for both of us. She appreciates therefore that she must not give any impression of singling me out for special favours or attention. Secrecy comes easily to Céline, *pas de problème*, so on one

134

level at least, that of appearances, I feel reasonably secure. However, the nights are long and often I have difficulty falling asleep, anxious that at any moment under cover of darkness she may steal into my room when my powers of resistance are at their lowest ebb. Sometimes even in day-time when I catch her oriental fragrance, despite my resolve to resist her, I yearn to feel her tremulous flesh and enter the luscious ripe fig of her body again.

While we were in Paris and had settled into a weekly rhythm together I barely considered what might become of us in the future. I suppose if Céline had stayed on with me I should merely have renewed the lease of my apart-ment so that we could continue as before, but the idea of a permanent relationship hadn't occurred to me. Nor had I thought for a minute of bringing her back to England with me, instinctively perhaps, aware as I have long been that links made with people abroad, say when you are on holiday, have a habit of snapping if you try to re-establish them on your home ground. They are a bit like those country wines which have so pleasant a tang when you drink them in Tuscany or Provence but lose their savour once they cross the Channel.

When at last I returned home alone from Paris I entered a domain which was familiar enough but at a standstill. There was evidence of Arabella throughout our house, but without the sound of her movements, her voice, her laughter, it lacked any heartbeat. I drifted from one empty room to the next and found it impossible to settle in any of them, like a rootless traveller who wanders disconsolately from place to place. I had lost a sense of purpose as well as my bearings, and so when I fell down the stairs that night it was as if I had leaped from a void where life was no longer tolerable yet without counting the cost of my severance from so much that had gone before.

10

I am relieved to have caught up to some extent with the cycle of events that preceded my arrival at Saxton House. However, I am left wondering if I might have excluded Céline altogether from my narrative to date but for her unexpected arrival here. It is not that I have sought deliberately to blot her out of my mind but that she was never a part of my life in England, where my revived memories of Arabella soon took hold, pushing aside most other thoughts, including any lingering reflections on my sweet-and-sour affair.

As it happens, Céline has come into my room several times while I have been writing almost exclusively about her. For spells of two or three minutes she ogles me as if keeping watch over an egg on the boil, but I don't look up. It is a rather droll situation to be in, to say the least. I think she is mildly curious as to what I am doing but seemed satisfied when I fed her a white lie and said that I am putting together some 'early reminiscences'. That's nice, she said, as if I am basket weaving, knitting a dish-cloth or sketching the wrinkling contents of my fruit-bowl. I don't think she'll nose around when I am out of my room, for as I said she is not a person who cares much for reading, but I am taking precautions by tucking away my accumulating notebooks just the same.

She has been quite forthcoming, in her own fashion, as to the circumstances that brought her here. She said she did go back to Paris for a while, and: 'Of course I went almost straight away to the Rue du Bac. My heart was thumping loud as I went up the stairs, I can tell you. Oh, how I wanted to see you, *mon bien-aimé*! How I'd missed you! There was no one for me to talk to, no one there to comfort me. So I phoned a friend, a girl I knew from before in London, and she said I could stay with her while I looked for a job. It was when I was there, in her flat, that I read the advertisement for a nurse. Mrs Durrance interviewed me in London and I liked her so much I agreed to come and work here without seeing the place. I wanted to get away from being in another big city, you see ... and, well, *voilà*, here I am. *Je crie au miracle.* Do you not agree that that is what it is?'

It is a miracle I could have done without, my dear. Our affair was unresolved, as such relationships often are, yet it was better that way. Things are different now, don't you see? I feel different; I do not seek the same stimulants, not for the present anyhow. I find your attempts to ingratiate yourself with me merely tedious, a bit pathetic too, occasional rushes to the head notwithstanding.

'You certainly took me by surprise – and not for the first time,' I respond spikily. I don't want Céline to steer me into any little *échange de confidences* as she would like. And immediately I regret my gratuitous barb 'and not for the first time'. The vaguely complicitous innuendo won't be lost on her.

Suddenly she starts to cry. Her little body seems to quiver all over and then comes a torrent of tears, gushing almost to order as from a squeezed doll. She whimpers uncontrollably. I should like to put my arms round her as all my instincts tell me to do, but I resist the impulse. 'What's the matter, Céline? What's the problem?' I ask woodenly, disquieted just the same by her rush of emotion.

Minutes go by before she calms down. Then I give her

137

a handkerchief to wipe her eyes and her cheeks. It is the least I can do.

Finally she says, haltingly: 'The matter ... *le problème* ... it is that you are so ... so distant with me, so *lointain*. You speak to me as if I am a stranger, someone you do not know. It has been like this all the time I am here. It was such a surprise to me, such a wonderful surprise, to find you here in this tiny village miles from anywhere ... it was *merveilleux*. And then I thought we could be like it was when we were together *en Paris*, when we shared *so much* ... that was good, *ce n'est pas*? I loved it *so much*, you know...'

'Until you went off without *so much* as a word...'

'But I told you why I left – *mon papa* ... he died. It was so sudden.' She dabbed her eyes. 'I was in shock, you know ... I just packed up and caught the first flight to Saigon ... I should have told you, yes, that was a mistake. *J'ai fait une erreur ... une grande erreur.* But it is not the end of the world to make such a mistake, *sûrement*? Please, can you not forgive me, Michel? ... I do not know what more I can say to you about this ... if you do not forgive me ... if you do not wish to understand.... *Je suis bien embarrassée....*' Her voice trailed almost into a whisper.

Subterfuge, half-truths, lies – I understand you, Céline. These things come naturally to you, you are unaware of their impact on someone else, like me for instance. Habitual liars like you, do you see, give themselves away by simple inconsistency. One minute they speak to impress, or to appease, or just to evade an issue, and ten minutes later or less, forgetting what they said in the first place, they contradict themselves. Even quite intelligent people do so. It is as if they don't trouble to listen to what they say, as if they are deaf to their own voices.

Or: Very well, Céline, I'll try to understand. I realise you probably meant no harm, not to me anyway, but I was concerned about you. More than anything, I was concerned for your safety.... You appeared to be living on the edge of a possible threat, of danger. I never pressed you about it but I was aware of it nevertheless. Remember how we met? You came running to me for help. You were running from the police – there was quite a posse of them looking for you in the gardens. I shall never forget it. You can't have forgotten it either. And then there was the mysterious jewel-case, the mysterious *empty* jewel-case, you said you were looking after for a friend. What was in that case? Did you ever discover? Did you ever trouble to look inside even once to see? Certainly you didn't seem to mind when you found it was empty. That was odd, surely? And what about the robbery in the Rue de Médicis on the very day you were running away from the police? Did you think I couldn't put two and two together, figure out for myself what occurred that morning in the Jardin du Luxembourg? Do you take me for a fool? And when finally you disappeared from my apartment, it happened to be the day after one of the thieves escaped. Were you nervous about that? Did it put you in fear of your life? Isn't that the real reason why you packed up and left Paris in such a hurry? Can you look me full in the face and answer just that one single question truthfully, Céline?

That's what I might have said if I had had the stomach for it, the guts; that's what I should have tried to say in so many words, if toned down somewhat. But with Céline I always thought, I still think, what would be the point? She forgets what she doesn't wish to remember. As I have thought all along, you have to accept her as she is. She isn't going to turn herself inside out for me or anyone else. In certain respects she resembles some creature of the wild living on its instincts and purely for survival, and there was never a bird or beast with a conscience, never mind Pavlov's dogs and those tinkling bells which reminded

139

them that they were hungry. Stroke her and she will purr, feed her and she will sing. You must leave it at that.

'There is nothing to forgive, Céline,' I said at last, anxious to stem another fountain of tears. 'Naturally I was concerned for you, but there it is. I shan't try to press you for any more explanations, you can be sure of that.'

She looked relieved if not mollified. I felt sorry for her but detached. I can't abide tears. Though they can jab you like needlepoints I reject the pain for which they agitate as well as express. Fortunately just then we were interrupted. Alice entered and asked for Céline's help to lift Doris Ashtead, who had slipped out of her bed on to the floor. She gave us a quick quizzical look which she swiftly disguised under her busy nurse's manner. She would have noticed that Céline was upset. You can tell very easily when someone has been crying, and besides, Céline was still clutching my large handkerchief. But she pulled herself together and half-smilingly muttered something about 'catching Michel's hay fever'. Her use of 'Michel' itself seemed rather a give-away, but then that would be quite natural coming from someone who is half French, and on that account Alice may have given her the benefit of the doubt if momentarily she suspected some intimacy between us. However, I think this is unlikely, Céline's proneness to gilding the lily invariably having the opposite effect to the one she intends. Yet I was uneasy that I had less concern for the source of Céline's tears than of discovery by another of the link between us.

Trudi Harrigan was quick to latch on to the fact that Céline and I already knew each other when, caught off guard on one occasion, I stupidly forgot to call her Jacqueline – or Jackie, as she is generally known. I tried to cover up my indiscretion (well, both names have the same final syllable) but Trudi is too alert to such nuances to be hoodwinked. So I filled her in briefly, without mentioning the vital jewel-case or bracelet, and she was at once sympathetic and said she would hug my confidence to herself. We had a good old natter about what a small world it is and she said it was just this kind of coincidence that was grist to the mill when she was spinning her yarns. Probably she would be more skilled at spinning this one than I am if she were given the full facts, or rather the facts as I know them. They are by no means as full as they might be, certainly so far as Céline is concerned.

Rosie's desertion by Denbigh is no longer under wraps. None of us knows for certain, but it seems that the runaway couple, in hiding for weeks, are now holed up in some shack on one of the Greek islands. Divorce proceedings, I gather, are already in hand. Rosie could of course divorce Denbigh on any number of pretexts – trainspotting, perhaps, even blowing his station-master's whistle too long and too loud, or squandering the housekeeping on maintaining his mini-collection of vintage cars which he kept buffed to a high sheen in the converted stables at the back of the coach-house and in one of which he occasionally emerged to attend some old-car rally or, when the mood took him, simply drove for the sheer hell of it with all the frenzy of some mad baddie from the same era as one of his prize motors, say a svelte Carl Peterson on the run from a hirsute Bulldog Drummond. In spite of or because of it all Rosie seems calmer now, is more relaxed, and it must be a comfort to her to have such obvious moral support from both the staff and the residents. Denbigh endeared himself to no one and consequently none of us misses him skulking around with the rations and so on. Village pets, moreover, will be able to enjoy a new lease of life now his old-world throttles stand silent.

I was thinking about Denbigh yesterday afternoon when I strolled by the coach-house. Rosie was outside in her front garden, busy with secateurs, and she greeted me with a friendly wave of her arm. 'Wonderful day,' she said.

'Yes, isn't it.'

I stopped by the wrought-iron gate.

'Would you come in for a minute, Michael?' she said. 'We can sit at the back in the garden. It's cooler there in the shade.'

'Yes, of course.'

I walked round the coach-house with Rosie and we seated ourselves more or less side by side in wooden chairs beside a round garden table set on paving-stones, surrounded by a small rockery in full flower. Bees throbbed amid the lavender.

'I've been wanting to have a chat with you for some time, but what with one thing and another.... You won't mind if I speak bluntly to you?'

My ears went back. My God, someone must have blabbed to her about me and Céline.

'No.'

'Well, to get straight to the point, you see it seems to me,' she went on, 'that your time of convalescence is over really. You cut a very different figure these days from the one you presented when you first came to us, I need hardly say. For one thing, you're walking unaided and quite normally now.'

I nodded.

'And your back is much better, isn't it?'

'Yes it is. I've discarded my corset, as you know, though of course I was glad of it for a while.'

'Yes. Good. Anyway it is always there if ever you feel the need of it again.'

'Yes.'

I rather anticipated what was coming next. I should

142

have much preferred dodging the issue. How pleasant it would have been just sitting there listening to the circling bees, daydreaming, the world's cares far away, Rosie with her pink body near enough to touch. Crescents of sweat swam like twin fish under the armpits of her bleached cotton dress.

'Now in one sense I don't want you to feel I am pushing you, but on the other hand I do urge you – well, I think you should seriously consider leaving us. You've been through a bad time, terrible – your wife's death and then your accident, and then that unfortunate tumble you had down the stairs here. I'm well aware of all that. But you don't need to be so dependent on others any more. In fact you hardly need us at all. I'll be perfectly frank, Michael, and I don't mean to be rude when I say that Saxton House isn't a hotel or a holiday home. Heaven forbid! In a nutshell, you're quite capable of looking after yourself, and I don't think you'll be doing yourself any good by lingering on here. Sooner or later – and best sooner – you ought to face up to this ... I feel this very strongly, for your own good and, well, my own peace of mind.'

Rosie looked at me intently while she was speaking. Her tone was emphatic but she kept her voice soft and low and I had to strain my ears to catch everything she was saying. When she added 'for my own peace of mind' I thought I detected a nostalgic expression steal across her face. I felt touched and was conscious simultaneously of her sexual heat held in check but simmering. She has a voluptuous appeal and it crossed my mind to take the plunge and ask her to come to bed with me then and there. But she cut me short.

'Had you met Jackie before?' she asked. She had caught me off balance – partly by her use of that name, to which I had never quite adjusted – but I quickly recovered.

143

'Yes, in Paris,' I replied vaguely, affecting unconcern.

'I thought so, somehow, but I've never mentioned it to Jackie. I didn't want her to think I was prying. What does shine out is, well, her special concern for your welfare.... I must say she's very good and has settled in here nicely. Gets on well with the others, and the other patients like her too. Sybil has taken a great fancy to her. She's partial to the Chinese, she told me, having lived in Hong Kong for a time after the war when Caspar served as an ADC to the Governor. They make such *loyal servants*, she thinks – her words not mine. Anyway I made the right choice taking Jackie on, and I just hope she'll stay with us....' Then after a pause she asked: 'Have you given any thought as to where you might go when you do leave here? I know you said you might decide to live permanently in France....'

I wondered if Rosie's wish for me to leave Saxton House and her desire for Céline to remain there were connected. It crossed my mind that she might be jealous of us – that remark about Céline's 'special concern' for my welfare, as she put it, was loaded. Frankly, I didn't care.

'Yes, I have given it a lot of thought but I've not come to any conclusion. You're quite right, of course, to say that it's time for me to move on. I've been putting off making a decision but I'll start thinking about it again in view of what you say – which I do appreciate.'

She leaned forward and pressed my hand. 'You know I only have your best interests in mind,' she said.

'Yes. Yes, I know.'

Did she really mean 'at heart'? Perhaps I could move in to the coach-house, I thought with sensual aplomb as a puff of Rosie's inviting odour drifted towards me. It might save me a lot of agonising. I felt I was becoming more and more indecisive as the days wore on.

She got up from her chair. 'Well, I suppose I must finish my bit of gardening before I go back to the salt-mines,'

144

she said with a small laugh. 'I'm glad we've had our talk. It's understood, isn't it Michael, that I don't want to rush you into anything?'

'Yes. Thank you.'

'Good. Give me some warning as soon as you do come to a decision. As usual, we've got many more people applying to come here than we have room for.'

After I left the coach-house I continued my stroll through the village. By the time I returned to Saxton House half an hour later I had virtually made up my mind, much to my own surprise, what to do. However, certain events that followed in quite quick succession conspired to stand my resolution on its head.

11

It was a couple of weeks after I had had my chat with Rosie that I noticed the stranger. Although the village of Saxton is off the beaten track, in the summer months you do see a few tourists walking around, by intent or accident you can't tell, but they always stand out from the local people. Generally they gravitate towards the Hereward Arms, as there is not much for them to look at except a few picture-postcard cottages and the Norman church, which in these days of roving vandals is usually kept locked.

The man, I would say he was in his mid-fifties, was sitting up at the bar by himself drinking a glass of white wine. He was plumpish and probably of middle to average height, so far as I could tell, with a round rather pug-like face and a receding hairline. He wore a long-sleeved pink check shirt, smart cream linen trousers with a multicoloured fabric belt and buckled brown shoes. Occasionally, when not sipping his wine, he turned his wrist to glance at his slim, elegant gold watch with a gold mesh strap, the gesture coinciding with a spatter of a leathery Hermès scent despatched like spindrift in my direction. I heard him exchange a few words, flat pleasantries, with the landlord behind the bar. He spoke quickly with a foreign accent of whose origin I couldn't be certain, yet almost at once I recognised him. Without doubt he was Céline's ex-lover, André. I say 'ex', but that is probably wishful thinking. He could hardly have stumbled upon Saxton like some of the other seasonal tourists but must have headed straight for it like a bear to a honey-pot. It was true that he did have a look of Charles Boyer, more so than of say Charlie Chaplin or Buster Keaton, though he was hardly his double as Céline had suggested. That was just one of her eager filmic simplifications or fantasies. Yet, whether or not one welcomed his arrival on the scene, at least he existed, and what Céline had said about him could be more or less verifiable.

As I stood at the bar with a glass of beer I toyed with the idea of introducing myself. The ugly thought crossed my mind that I might then remark casually and cruelly to Céline, taking the wind out of her sails, 'As I was saying to André, you are so clever with cushions', or 'You do wonders with sheepskin rugs.' But whatever the vulgarities of one's thoughts, such male chauvinistic pique is best kept to oneself. Besides, I might never know if Céline had invited André to visit her in England or whether he had actually come of his own volition, taking up where he had left off so to speak, if ever he had withdrawn his advances, which I now rather doubted.

I wasn't at all happy with this situation. In a sense it had nothing to do with me, it was none of my business. Céline was free to do what she liked, for I had tried to make it plain that, so far as I was concerned, my relationship with her was a thing of the past. Yet I had the feeling that she meant to play one or other of us, meaning André and me, against the other. And conceit urged me to think that I was the one on whom she intended to try out her ruse of emotional blackmail. Did she know me better than I knew myself? When Céline had parted from me in Paris I must have lived on in her mind as she had done in mine. We still carried traces of one another that we had left behind, imprints that were ineradicable whether one liked it or not. By means of these Céline could be as wise to me as I was to her. I might spy on her in my mind's eye as through a one-way mirror, but I should be mistaken in imagining that, when it suited her, she could not do precisely the same in reverse and hold me up to the light for close inspection like a framed photograph of an old lover – old in both senses of the word.

I'd barely had time to thrash out these farraginous thoughts, to brood about alternative courses of action, than Céline herself entered the pub, not in uniform but off-duty clothes – a striped yellow T-shirt and faded blue jeans. As she caught sight of the pair of us poised at opposite corners of the bar like ill-matched book-ends, I could tell she was momentarily taken aback. Embarrassed is too strong a word for it, and anyway as I said earlier Céline in her natural guise of inscrutable oriental never betrayed any hint of such disquiet. She was disconcerted simply because our unexpected presence together must have wrong-footed her, pre-empting whatever provocative scheme she may surreptitiously have devised. Am I attributing to Céline deceits she never intended? No, I think not. I think she has always been well aware of what she is doing, however apparently spontaneous her actions.

Quickly recovering her composure and beaming her brightest smile she introduced André and me to each other. André looked somewhat surprised and stood up from his stool as I made a point of going over and shaking his spongy hand, formally but not stiffly, in the correct continental manner. Céline showed her hand, I thought, though in a different way, by her sudden though measured use of 'Michael' rather than 'Michel' and by then explaining that I was 'a patient' (using Rosie's term) at Saxton House. She kept our surnames out of her introduction in the way that young people often do, though it seemed to me that in this case hers was a careful

148

omission, deliberate in order to strike a note of casualness and possibly in an attempt to conceal André's identity from me. In any event I sensed that my name, the English version anyhow, signified nothing to André, and intuitively Céline must have counted on my discretion, that is to say that I wouldn't disclose any foreknowledge of his blinking star in her arcane galaxy of admirers. Oh yes, you're the wanker banker from the Hôtel Crillon, kind of thing.

When I say Céline showed her hand by calling me Michael, I mean that she was distancing herself from me so that André's ears wouldn't prick up and catch a note of familiarity between us, for such is the way of lovers with their keen senses, twitchingly as alert as antennae probing the air. In other words, she didn't appear to have had it in mind to play me against him, though maybe the opposite was the case, as I had suspected.

She sat up on a bar-stool between us, almost purring with feline contentment at having the undivided if passing attention of her two errant suitors. André offered her a drink and she said yes, she'd love one, she was very thirsty. The heat, you know. So he ordered her a sweet vermouth with ice and soda and a slice of lemon. It was what she often had on hot summer days in the Rue du Bac, I recalled; not a taste acquired from me but evidently familiar to André too, since he had raised his bushy eyebrows and said 'The usual?'

'*Vous êtez en vacances ici?*' I asked speciously, as though he could as easily have percolated through the ancient stones of the Hereward Arms like an indigenous fungus.

Céline turned to me and explained that André was an old friend of hers from Paris, though he lived now in Geneva. Surprise surprise.

'*Oui*, I am 'ere to enjoy the English countryside for a few days. I ev been first on business in London and then Céline ver' kindly invited me to stay in 'er place, but it is *un peu petit*' – he affected an awful grin, more of a grimace, revealing a glint of gold-capped teeth, a cloud of his Hermès scent enveloping me – 'so I ev *une chambre*, a room, in the 'ereward.... It is *très simple* but fine. I am quite comfortable and I ev a car, rented from the garage, to drive 'ere and there....'

He sounded like a talking machine, trotting out his dreary sentences as if newly culled from some banal English phrase-book. Charles Boyer my foot. Céline meanwhile sat alternately smiling and sipping her drink, her almond eyes darting back and forth between us like an umpire following the flight of a ball between contestants at a tennis match.

André asked me a few conventional questions about Saxton House, to which I replied as politely and informatively as I could. He carefully avoided any reference to my own actual state of health, Céline would doubtless tell him as much as he wanted to know about that in due course, but I did let drop the fact that I wouldn't be staying on much longer. As I did so, I stole a glance at Céline. But though she kept her smile in place, her expression was otherwise impassive, as I should have expected it to be. In fact this was the first time I had suggested anything in front of her about my leaving the nursing home. It was my way of sending her a message, stealing a march on her – yes, cocking a snook if you like: taunt me as you will, play on my vulnerability, my jealousy, I still have my own private agenda. It was the old cat-and-mouse stratagem, which would not be lost on her, not for a minute. Céline knew all the shots in the love war.

I say 'love war' because I intuited that, however deliberately I had set out to detach myself from Céline, to cut the clinging vine, the presence of another man, in André's case a sexual partner, was enough to disinter feelings of possessiveness towards her I had half imagined were as dust. In that regard I had been fooling myself all along. A part of me had self-protectively wished to be rid of her. I had had enough of anxieties and uncertainties; I couldn't bear the thought of being left in the lurch again. Nor did I relish being as putty in a young girl's hands; I liked to be in command. How subtly had Céline read me! This was all the more reason why I should resist her challenge to my emotional integrity. I must press home the moral advantage I had fleetingly gained by my nonchalantly saying that I intended to quit Saxton House. I must seize the initiative if not effect a *coup de maître*.

'Céline loves picnics, you know,' I said to André while smiling winningly at Céline. 'Don't you, *ma chérie*? Why don't you take her for one, André, now we have this lovely warm weather?'

'That is a good idea,' he replied woodenly and without conviction, raising his bushy eyebrows again as he turned his head enquiringly towards Céline, who gave a wan smile and looked down into her lap.

'It was one of Céline's favourite pastimes when we both lived in Paris and she's always asking me to take her on an outing here.'

'*Outing?*'

'I mean, take her out on a picnic.'

'Ah *oui*, I understand.'

It was a wretched thing to do. At one and the same time I was sewing seeds of doubt in André's mind and firing Cupid's arrow – leaden rather than golden, the distinction should be made – at Céline. Clearly I was confusing them both in quite different ways.

'You lived in Paris, *oui?*'

'Yes,' I said, cutting across Céline, who looked as if she were about to intervene in an effort to cover her tracks and maybe mine as well. 'I lived there for about eighteen months. It must have been after you had returned to

Geneva.' I turned to Céline. 'Isn't that so?' I asked, addressing her and as though to emphasise that André's life was an open book that held no secrets for me.

Céline didn't reply but tilted her glass, gently rattling the remaining ice inside and then looking carefully at it like a laboratory assistant examining tonsils in a bottle.

'*Un autre?*' André asked her.

'*Merci.*' She shook her head.

There was an awkward silence which I made no effort to break. I was enjoying my psychological vantage-point, having ruffled the feathers of *les oiseaux d'amour*, as I mockingly chose to see them, as with a cat's claw – a tom-cat's at that. Physical jealousy can be paralysing, yet how it can drive a man, how inspiratorial it can be. It is an affliction that excites no fear save obliquely of loss, of betrayal. It can make a demon of a minion, switch on the action in the theatre of one's mind. One moment you may be like an anaemic young actor sitting before the looking-glass in his dressing-room, a make-up artist applying finishing touches to his visage while a dresser adjusts his helmet, the next the selfsame thespian is metamorphosed into monarch, heroic icon, as he exhorts the poor condemned English from his sinewy charger, the breath from its nostrils vaporising the chill morning air of Agincourt. Here at the Hereward Arms where the three of us sat swivelling on our bar-stools, each of us in our own way an outcast of love, we continued our own private charade; yet deep down how sick I was in my lassitude of feeling forced into playing the role of manipulative cynic, spoiling the little manoeuvre of romantic cajolery Céline had attempted from her need of a man (either André or me, it wasn't clear which one of us; perhaps she needed us both), and rattling André, a complete stranger to me and no less a willing captive of her charms than I had been.

It was physical jealousy that had spurred me on, regardless of whom I wounded in the stagy arena Céline had unwittingly devised. I felt impelled to fight my corner. Dismissive as I had been of André as a rival, I dared not contemplate Céline appropriating his member with her inimitable finesse. As she sat in silence between us we each took her by a hand as if staking a claim on her person. It was puerile behaviour but understandable, I think, in these curiously competitive circumstances. I have no idea what expression I wore on my face but I could see that André looked distinctly ill at ease. There was sweat on his domed forehead and he had a fishy look in his eyes, which he trained on Céline in an attempt I imagined to ignore my presence altogether.

'Another glass of wine, André?' I said, trying to wrest his attention.

'No thank you, *monsieur*,' he replied politely but coldly, barely glancing in my direction.

I pressed Céline's hand and said, '*Qu'est-ce que tu prends, ma chérie? Un vermouth?*' We might just as well all speak in snippets of French if that was the way André wanted it.

She shook her head and let go of my hand, or rather removed hers from mine, and then almost simultaneously took her other hand from André's. She must have been well aware of the tension she was creating between André and me, which of course I myself had set in motion with my hint of a shared love-nest in Paris once he was out of sight, having flown back like a visitant serenading cuckoo to his domestic habitat. I dare say that for his part he could have been agonising about my member as I had about his, and with no less distaste. I had no doubt we shared a terrible male pride, now to the fore as a consequence of our having enjoyed the same delectable mistress.

Out of desperation probably, in an effort to steer us out of our sticky impasse, Céline launched with almost tipsily exaggerated enthusiasm into the subject of art, of paintings. Nothing too specific, I thought thankfully, because there can be no more moribund topic to introduce among strangers, but in her own ingenuous way I expect she was trying to tell André and me that we might have some interest in common apart from herself.

Adumbrating my own reaction, André clutched at this straw with evident relief and began a long-winded exposition, speaking in French, of the work of some of the Italian Renaissance masters whom evidently he set above all other painters of every other period. He was dismissive of the Impressionists, describing them *en bloc* as mere absinthe-infused *barbouilleurs*, daubers, he repeated the word with disdain, a contentiousness I chose to ignore. However, I continued listening with glazed inattentiveness, ever since my schooldays lectures of any kind have made me feel dozy, and I was glad when eventually the rubicund landlord (not a local man but a townee given to simulating the hearty rustic) intervened and said gruffly, probably thinking this trio of art fanciers with their fancy French a touch hoity-toity, that it was time gentlemen please. He might appositely have added 'Seconds out of the ring', since the closing of the bar would effectively terminate the sham truce Céline had rigged between what she may out of simple vanity have conceived as her punchdrunk paramours.

I stood up. The others remained seated, apparently expecting me to go. Perhaps André would invite Céline to his room, though that seemed unlikely under the tacky gaze of the landlord. He surely wouldn't want to compromise her so openly because of her link with the nursing home. A man from his station in life, a big shot at a bank, would presumably have a code of some kind; tailored manners.

He said *au revoir* to me courteously, though implying

154

with a wry look, Don't hang around. Scram. *Allez au diable.*

'*Bonne journée,*' I responded. And then: '*Bonnes vacances.*' Stuff him, I thought.

I had a throbbing headache, the after-effects of beer and from the explosion of summer heat, perhaps exacerbated by emotional tension, so I went straight to my room, took two aspirins and lay down on my bed. I was both depressed and dissatisfied with the way I had behaved. It wasn't so much a question of what I had or hadn't said either to André or to Céline but of my attitude towards them, which, despite an air of languor I had self-protectively assumed, was malicious, bordering on hostility. If I had truly rejected Céline, why should I object to her liaison with André? If I didn't wish to keep her for myself, I should be willing to let her go. I couldn't have it both ways.

I fell into a deep sleep for I don't know how long. So blank was the dark of my insensibility I could have been dead. When – one hour, two hours later? – I woke up, I was surprised to find Céline sitting at my bedside. She looked fearfully pale, her skin was waxen, and her eyes were dull, misted over, though they glimmered when I sat up and looked at her sad face.

Oh my poor darling, whither your dreams?

'I love you,' I said.

We sat quite still in a fold of silence as though listening for the splash from the plunge I had taken.

'*Moi aussi. Je t'adore.*'

I rose from my bed and when Céline stood up I held her close in my arms. Her gracile fingers pressed at my waist, tenderly, expectant.

'Then will you marry me?' I asked after a while. No, I

didn't blurt it out. Rather, the words bubbled forth pure and evergreen as from the Pierian spring.

I felt her tremble and she stared up at me with such rapture I knew for certain what her answer would be, if ever I could have doubted it for an instant. An almost imperceptible cry escaped her lips.

'Yes,' she said. '*Oh, yes.*'

12

The weekly piano recitals given by Ingrid Mackintosh have become a regular feature of life at Saxton House, to which even the less musically minded among the residents eagerly look forward. This excitement, previously rare in the home, is in happy contrast to their lethargic response to television, in front of whose constant glow in the sitting-room their ageing eyelids flap and droop like tired moths. It all began following the day I heard Ingrid playing a Beethoven sonata. She took my advice and asked Rosie if she would be prepared to acquire a supply of musical scores, which she could not herself afford, an idea which gladdened Rosie and to which she responded with alacrity. Thereafter, usually on Fridays around teatime, Ingrid has performed for a good half-hour or so, sometimes longer, though she has to be careful about extending the length of her recitals, she says, else her hands start stiffening up. Not only has her playing given us all infinite pleasure, it has transformed Ingrid's whole personality in our midst, like the revival of a wilting plant from fresh water. Once dour and suspicious, she has opened up and become quite chatty, ready to share some of her thoughts with the rest of us. Her repertoire is classical – mainly pieces by Schubert, Beethoven, Chopin, at which she is adept – but she is no musical snob and is always ready to respond to a particular request, say for a popular melody, so long as she has the score.

For Sybil Ayres-Southey's ninetieth birthday Ingrid was

asked to give a special concert, consisting of old dance tunes and songs from musicals chosen by Sybil herself. 'I should like a light little musical soufflé but whisked with passion,' she remarked, the merest blush of a smile re-animating her once irresistible lips. The celebration began at teatime with a splendid cake Rosie had had specially made for the occasion, its white icing adorned with the words *Happy Birthday Sybil* in pink within a circlet of red roses and topped by nine pink candles. After Sybil had managed with Caspar's help to blow out the candles (the effort turned Caspar's face a deeper shade of pink) and the cake had been cut and we had all had a nibble, we sat more or less facing in the direction of the piano, Rosie and some of the nurses, Alice, Susan, Ben and Céline among them, standing in a semicircle in the background, spilling into the front room. It had been quite hot earlier on, but there was now a benign breeze swishing through the open windows, a welcome inflow with such a gather-ing, almost a full complement of residents and staff in fact as normally occurs only on Christmas Day.

At last Ingrid struck a chord – C, *ping* – then played a few bars as a means of introducing the first melody, turn-ing her head as she did so towards Sybil, who was seated close by the piano with Caspar.

At this point Rosie suddenly intervened. 'I think we should all thank Ingrid for agreeing to play to us today,' she pronounced in her best headmistress tone.

There came a dutiful clapping of hands as at a prize-giving ceremony. Ingrid gave a shy, slanting smile of acknowledgement.

'And now let us first sing "Happy Birthday".'

Rosie, slightly flushed, her mouth half open in a frozen smile, bobbed her head in that clucking-chicken way of hers towards Ingrid. Whereupon we all joined in with fair gusto. I was standing beside Tim Follaton, with whose deep baritone I was familiar from our homespun Sunday services, and I wondered if perhaps he might do a solo. He'd be good with Gilbert and Sullivan, I thought. But as I was to find out, their jolly airs were not to be included in the programme that now commenced.

The emphasis of this was on music of the twenties, thirties and forties, Noël Coward and Ivor Novello prominent among the composers, romantic and sentimental all of it, to be sure – there was no *Yeah! Yeah! Yeah!* about it – and cloying probably to some modern ears, yet no less cogent to us old-timers.

'I never realised what you were to me.
I never realised that such a thing could be.
But when you went away dear, then I was sad, because
I never realised what a fool I was...'

While Sybil herself sang these words by heart, quaveringly, with some diffidence, as though anxious not to steal too much of the limelight, like a reluctant belle of the ball, I threw a glance at Céline across the room, eyeing her in a knowing way like those heroes do their womenfolk in certain old Hollywood movies of the kind so beloved by Céline. And after all I was her *pimprenelle* again, ready to limber up for the chandeliers.

I suppose we were about half-way through the concert when Megan Rees got to her feet and asked Sybil, who was sitting next to her, if she could make a request. 'Of course, whatever you like, Megan,' Sybil replied graciously.

'Then I'd like "Land of My Fathers",' said Megan. ' "*Hen Wlad fy Nhadau*",' she chirruped through a gash of a smile.

This was rather out of key, or harmony, with the rest of the programme, to say the least, but Sybil responded, this time with some vehemence, 'But *of course*, my dear.'

Then, to Ingrid at the piano, she asked: 'Do you know this Welsh song, Ingrid?' Ingrid shook her head. 'Well, don't let that inhibit us,' said Sybil. 'We'll give you a lead.' Sybil nodded to Megan. 'I'm afraid I don't really know the words,' she said, 'but if you'd like to start us off, Megan, we'll all join in – won't we?' she asked, inclining her head towards the rest of us. There was a murmur of general assent.

Megan looked very excited, almost overwhelmed by suddenly becoming the focus of attention. 'I'll do my best,' she said sweetly, shyly, and then she leaned over and planted a kiss on Sybil's forehead. Sybil shone a glad smile back at her. Then in a thin, piping voice, like that of a reedy choirboy, Megan began to sing the rousing anthem which always seems to roll down from the blue and mauve Welsh hills. Soon the room swelled with a humming and chanting, and then Ingrid chimed in on the piano as though she had known the tune all her life.

When Megan had sat down there was a warm round of applause. I wondered irreverently if Trudi Harrigan beside me might now ask for 'The Battle Hymn of the Republic', but if the thought crossed her mind she must have quickly stifled it. She looked quietly amused though she had barely joined in any of the singing, contenting herself with more or less speaking in her crackly voice some of the words to 'Can't Help Lovin' That Man' and Cole Porter's 'I Get a Kick Out of You'.

As Ingrid played a few introductory chords of 'Some Enchanted Evening', Sybil, addressing the menfolk, asked if one of us would volunteer to sing this favourite song of hers, though it must have postdated her courtship by Caspar. Tim was the only one among us with an authentic voice. Bill Budgett had earlier suffered an uncontrollable fit of coughing, that pipe of his, which had driven him purple-faced from the room; I need a supporting cast;

160

and schmaltzy lyrics were hardly young Ben's forte. Nor was Caspar really up to it, doubtless saving his wind for the major contribution he was to make later on.

'I'd be glad to oblige, Lady Sybil,' said Tim, getting up and making his way towards the piano, where he stood rugged, Victorian-looking, masterful, reading the music-sheet over Ingrid's shoulder.

'Some enchanted evening, you may see a stranger
You may see a stranger across a crowded room…'

He was doing well, the mellow timbre of his voice, grooved with his rustic intonation, giving a showbiz dimension to the song. Perhaps he should have gone on the stage, devoted his life to glamorous nights in front of rainbow footlights instead of having to stride across cold, wet fields, slicing through icy winds to tend his sodden cattle. Perhaps as he sang he was thinking back, remembering wistfully the girl who had rejected him all those years ago.

'Then fly to her side and make her your own…'

Clearly Caspar's flying days were over, but at this point he winged or rather plonked a hand on Sybil's forearm in a marionette-like gesture as he might once have rested a white gauntlet on the withers of his black mount. In response to which Sybil said with a snap in her voice, incisive enough to sever his extremity at the wrist, and loud enough momentarily to disconcert the singer, 'It's far too hot, Caspar.' For such nonsense, she might have added. Born to command he may have been, but Caspar now tamely withdrew his scaly fingers like the Obeisant Shrimp he had become, ever deferential, ever at his wife's beck and call.

161

Now came the finale. This was a duet performed appropriately by Sybil and Caspar. For their chosen tune, 'I'll Follow My Secret Heart' from Coward's *Conversation Piece*, they stood up, Caspar lending Sybil a supporting arm. They didn't need to consult the music-sheet, since they knew the words by heart. I wondered if they had rehearsed it beforehand, sung it perhaps in their younger days in the manner of Coward himself and his frisky leading lady Yvonne Printemps, conjecture which on this day of days had little relevance; horizons had shifted. They looked touching together, this once amorous couple, Caspar smiling and looking round the room benevolently in the manner of a famous performer, Sybil in her role of diva, star of her own show, a mottled hand resting lightly on her black pearls, her Zoglets, still in her frailty a queenly presence.

> 'A cloud has pass'd across the sun,
> The morning seems no longer gay,
> With so much bus'ness to be done
> Even the sea looks grey,
> C'est vrai! C'est vrai!'

While Caspar sang, or rather half muttered the words in a low growly sort of voice, from down in the foothills so to speak, Sybil went straight for the alpine heights. But the air at the summit was now too thin for her, and although she had the remnants of a fine voice, she emitted a rather strange, a rather eerie sound, not tra-la-la, not trilling exactly, more Wailing Wall. A splutter came from the front room. It was Ben, who had got the giggles. These were catching and, quickly caught by Susan, were in danger of spreading like an epidemic. But Rosie Durrance, alert to possible disruption, spun round and aimed a withering look at them, a scorched-earth kind of look that might have zapped them to extinction if they hadn't at once removed themselves from the line of fire and sidled cowering, still tittering, from the room.

Neither Sybil nor Caspar noticed any of this; rather, they had eyes only for each other.

> 'You ask me to have a discreet heart
> Until marriage is out of the way,
> But what if I meet with a sweetheart so sweet
> That my heart cannot obey
> A single word that you may say?'

What indeed. Caspar, not given to toeing the amatory line in his bouncing Blues period, may well have wrestled with as loaded a question. However, he now wore an almost adoring (or was it gaga?) expression as his watery eyes continued blinking up at Sybil's face, of which he could have lost focus without his spectacles, and he growled out the words *sotto voce* while Sybil, her voice dipping too, descending upon and sugaring Caspar's like icing on marzipan, like her own birthday cake, seemed suddenly to be peering above and beyond the upright piano as if towards some far-off vista. Then at last they tottered in tandem, a little breathlessly, into the final leg, let us say victory lap, of their impassioned duet, as of their lives.

> 'I'll follow my secret heart my whole life through
> I'll keep all my dreams apart till one comes true...'

It was to be Sybil's swan-song. The day after her birthday concert she had a heart attack. Whether this was circumstantial, brought on by the extra excitement of the previous afternoon's festivities or merely a chance happening that could have occurred at any time, in the doctor's opinion it was impossible to say. In any event, it was a severe attack, and although she lingered on for a few days, to begin with in a semiconscious state, during which she rallied at times and spoke quite coherently, even trenchantly in a wistful *grande dame* manner, within a week she was dead.

Everyone was shaken by this. In a home for the elderly death is a natural enough occurrence, though oddly Sybil was the first to succumb in all the time I had been at Saxton House. It was partly because she was snatched from us so soon after her birthday party, which was still uppermost in our minds. We were all fond of her, admired her, nurses as well as residents. It was to do with her unbowing spirit; her refusal to surrender in the face of her declining physical state, and no less in matters of social conduct, which came high in her list of priorities; her very Englishness. She could be acerbic, caustic, yet at the same time silkily self-mocking, and she was essentially kind, betraying at times her innate soft-heartedness, her romantic disposition – witness her choice of songs for her birthday concert.

Céline, who had nursed her towards the end, broke the news to me. She was very upset, her eyes were moist, not surprisingly since so strong a patient–nurse bond had developed between her and Sybil, of which Rosie had made me aware.

'She was a really lovely lady,' she said. 'She had a beautiful voice, too.'

I found this a bit hard to reconcile with poor Sybil's failing vocal powers, but then Céline's ears had once been attuned to the ethereal cadences of Chinese opera, with which, come to think of it, the notes in the *nella parte di sopra* of Sybil's ascendant scales seemed to have a strange affinity.

The funeral was a small private affair conducted in a neighbouring town, attended I gather by only a handful of relatives, a married niece and a nephew among them, since most of Sybil's contemporaries were either too old to attend or had already died. Rosie made it a rule not to go to the funerals of her former patients, partly because of their frequency, but Ben and Céline asked if they could accompany Caspar, helping the old man through a difficult day.

Caspar had at first appeared bemused by the events – bemused, I think, rather than stunned by them. To begin with, in the days immediately following the funeral, he kept to his room, though I am uncertain as to whether this was from personal choice or because Rosie had prevailed on him to lie low and rest thoroughly after all the recent strains and stresses he must surely have had to endure. Probably the latter. And maybe he was bemused partly because he had not previously come downstairs unaccompanied by Sybil. He must have been disorientated without her to take his arm, to escort into lunch and so forth, and if her manner towards him had often struck one as autocratic, if she had been remiss in neglecting to pass him the salt and pepper, a part of him had been hollowed out over the years to accept her intrusion into himself, through manipulation or from habit, in the way that in time a seashore accommodates the resurgence of eroding waves with an inlet or cave. Her withdrawal from his life, like a receding tide, had left in its wake a void, an empty cavern, relentlessly sucked dry by death.

Megan, Trudi and Ingrid each tried to fill this void by offering themselves as companions to Caspar. Nevertheless, while he was as polite to them as ever, as the days wore on he made it quietly apparent in his own unassuming fashion that he wasn't looking for a Sybil substitute, he had been in harness perhaps too long, but rather that he was more interested in the company of us menfolk, Bill Budgett in particular. The two of them began to discuss their army days at length, re-evaluating old battles fought and won or lost, such that the pepper and salt, which in the past had tended to evade Caspar's reach, began instead to be marched regularly up and down the dining-table, representing, along with certain pieces of cutlery, an assortment of military hardware, or on occasion erstwhile commanders directing operations among the spilled condiments as amidst shot and shell.

These martial exercises, or war games, left the women somewhat nonplussed, but they were tolerant of them, seeing them probably as a passing phase, and glad no doubt that Bill and Caspar, reticent with each other in the past (a matter of social rank?), had found so stimulating a bond.

All the while Sybil's presence seemed to hang over the smoke of battle like an amused spectre, a glint of her sardonic smile igniting our private reveries as the guns blazed.

13

Sybil, in her absence, with her long shadow, dominated my last days at Saxton House.

It was Rosie who first noticed that her pearls were missing. Sybil had last been seen wearing them at the concert. Had she removed them afterwards? If so, where had she put them? When questioned by Rosie the nurses in turn confirmed that though Sybil was never without them by day, she invariably took them off at night. Sometimes she placed them in a rather tatty cardboard box in the recess of her bedside table; at other times she liked to tuck them like a mascot or talisman under her pillow. The box was still there but it was empty. A thorough search of her room was made, the floor space under her bed was re-examined, her drawers gone through, but these had already been emptied and so her suitcases with her remaining clothes were opened up. Nothing. Then the vacuum-cleaner bag was emptied, even the washing machine was scrutinised, just supposing the pearls had somehow got caught up in her pillowcase, which had been put inside with her other bedclothes. Everything, all the searches, drew a complete blank.

So what on earth could have happened to them?

The key to the lost or mislaid pearls could be Caspar, Rosie intuited. Some key. Caspar was singularly indifferent as to their fate. 'Sybil's pearls? Sorry, I'm afraid I haven't the foggiest idea where she could have put them. Search me,' he said. He wasn't actually suggesting that a search was made there and then of his person, but there was no holding Rosie. She knew Caspar was vague. She knew a fog when she saw one. She knew that with his slipping memory he shared the debility of her other patients, it was part of the natural retrogression of old age, so she rummaged as tactfully as she could through his belongings, always neatly put away. He may have been forgetful, but he was personally fastidious.

A grim thought then came into her mind. Horror of horrors, supposing the pearls had been placed in Sybil's coffin, unnoticed by the undertakers, and then went the way of the whole caboodle to the crematorium? Were pearls resistant to fire?

Again all the nurses were summoned and questioned by Rosie. No, the pearls had definitely not been on Sybil's person when the 'funeral directors' called, she was told, though Alice and Céline, who had tended Sybil in her last hours, had removed her rings and, as Rosie well knew, she had been handed them for safe keeping with her other jewellery.

Reluctantly, as a somewhat desperate last-minute resort, Rosie telephoned the funeral parlour. They would initiate immediate enquiries, she was told. Within half an hour she was rung back and assured that no item of jewellery had been discovered on the body of her ladyship when they had laid her out, not even a wedding-ring. Of course if any piece of any kind had been found, it would have been put aside and Mrs Durrance would have been consulted straight away and asked for further instructions. They followed very strict procedures in all such matters. I had the impression that the undertakers were more than a little peeved that their integrity might have been called into question.

No one had reckoned on the intervention of possible beneficiaries of Sybil's will. There are always such people scratching about, lured by the hint of gold, their incisors grinding for a predatory bite. In this case it was Sybil's niece and nephew who came out of the woodwork. The offspring of Sybil's elder sister, who had died several years before, they had appeared briefly at the funeral, and they now arrived at Saxton House with the family solicitor. Sybil and Caspar had had no children and so Elspeth Tinburgh (wife of a diplomat, Sir Harry Tinburgh) and her brother Mark Strent were Sybil's nearest relatives, her sole unmarried brother having been killed in the war. In effect this meant that the family title was now extinct, since there was no male heir left to inherit it, the Alfrick earldom having to pass directly from father to son, an anomaly or cock-up (so Caspar said) that bore the hall-mark of some of the more random dispensations of Charles II. All this is by the way except to emphasise the potential influence or leverage Lady Tinburgh and her brother might bring into play when the chips were down.

The chips in this case, in a manner of speaking, as was quickly established by Elspeth Tinburgh, were 'the Zog pearls'. A tall, forceful woman in her fifties, who deferred only briefly to Caspar, she asked the solicitor to read the will. You could see certain family resemblances between Elspeth, Mark and Sybil, for instance in their fair complexions as well as in their facial features (those wide aristo nostrils) and bone structure, and in their general bearing too. Elspeth Tinburgh took the lead (shades of Sybil), whereas Mark Strent appeared to be of a retiring disposition, probably enlisted by his sister for moral support rather than because he had any personal expectations from the will.

Of course I wasn't a witness to what took place in private in Rosie's office, lent by Rosie for the reading of the will. I am simply putting the pieces together as best I can from what was repeated to me shortly afterwards, filtering through from Caspar to Rosie. Sybil had left all her remaining jewellery, for the most part family pieces specified in a clause in the will, entirely to her niece. This was duly checked, item by item, having been given by Rosie to the solicitor at his request for handing on to Elspeth after probate. One item, however, had been omitted altogether from the will, and this was the prize of prizes, namely the Zog pearls.

At this news Elspeth must have become very agitated. Her expectations had been dashed; she had been dealt a truly fearful blow. She grew angry, demanding to know what had become of the necklace. She then turned on Caspar, not accusingly quite but as much as to suggest that there was more behind this than met the eye. A conspiracy of some kind? The idea was absurd but her suspicions seemed to be confirmed when it was revealed that the necklace had disappeared. *Disappeared?* How could the pearls have *disappeared*?

The fact that Elspeth had no rightful claim to the pearls, effectively that what had or hadn't become of them was none of her business, was neither here nor there so far as she was concerned. Well, of course the necklace was priceless but, more, this was a 'family matter', indeed a matter of considerable family pride. After all, King Zog had been a great friend of her grandfather's; they must both be turning in their graves. One could not help reflecting later that Sybil, if unable to turn in her final resting-place, was having the last laugh.

Rosie was beckoned again to her office, Elspeth Tinburgh insisting that, since she, Mrs Durrance, had been unable to locate the missing necklace, she should send for the police without further ado. She was duty bound to do so; she owed it to Caspar, she added as an afterthought. There should be a full investigation forthwith.

Rosie, not normally one to bow under pressure, somewhat reluctantly agreed to Elspeth's request. The thought had already crossed her own mind, but she had dismissed it. The last thing she wanted was any sort of public scandal. The arrival of police at the home might itself be enough to set village tongues wagging, and these days there were always newspaper reporters with itchy fingers skulking in the bushes, television cameramen ready to zoom in and spotlight any speck of the censurable or scabrous. Yes she would, she assured Lady Tinburgh and Mr Strent, keep them posted through Lady Sybil's solicitor of any developments.

After which somewhat frenzied exchange the three visitors bade an aloof, official, probably frosty kind of goodbye and went on their way.

The police came and went too. They asked all the usual questions, cross-questioned each member of the staff individually, made extensive notes, requested a detailed description of the necklace, asked who King Zog was (Was he a black man? Well, black pearls, black king), implying in a plodding way that he sounded a right queer one, and what would a gentleman be doing with pearls? Rosie had told them that her patients were above reproach and consequently, and no doubt in deference to our ages, we were all treated with due circumspection and propriety. As for Caspar, he said he wondered why everyone was making such a song and dance about the wretched pearls – 'Sybil's baubles' he called them. 'Rather ugly, I always thought,' he muttered disparagingly, 'though of course Sybil was awfully attached to them.' There were some perhaps, those say of a more worldly disposition, who might have interpreted this remark as that of a man breasting senility. I believe they would have been wrong: Caspar meant what he said; his comment, if airy, carried personal conviction.

171

The eye of suspicion now fell on Céline. Certainly I had been left wondering about her possible involvement in the affair of the missing pearls, her very proximity to Sybil in her final hours inspiring the thought. None the less it didn't bear thinking about and, call me faint-hearted, I knew better than to try to question Céline myself.

The suspicion of the police seemed to have been aroused if not actively stimulated by Rosie, never mind her initial reluctance to provoke their attention. This struck me as uncharacteristically disloyal of her, acting as she had against her principles in singling out a member of her own staff, especially a nurse of whom she had spoken with such enthusiasm and who was so popular with the others. Moreover she had begun to adopt a rather hostile attitude towards Céline. 'We don't really know much about the girl or her background,' she was heard to complain intemperately. I couldn't help feeling that Rosie was being driven by some personal motive. Could it be me? Was she jealous of my relationship with Céline? Rosie had of course been aware for some time that I had known Céline before she came to work at Saxton House. However, since Céline and I had come quite recently together again, we had taken care not to behave indiscreetly at the home, and nor had we made known our unofficial engagement. But as I said earlier in relation to André, there is something between lovers, some current, that the watchful can sense, and Rosie was nothing if not intuitive to a high degree. I was aware that she had fancied me as I had fancied her, but apart from her one stolen kiss that afternoon in the coach-house she had made no move to entice me. Had she left it to me to take the next step? Was she disappointed that I had done little more to reveal the old Adam than salivate at the sight of her oozing armpits when we were having our little chat in her rock garden? I may never know the answer.

172

When the police telephoned to say that they were coming to collect Céline for further questioning at the station, she came rushing up to my room. 'Michel, you have got to rescue me,' she pleaded. They had already searched her room in the house where she was lodging, she informed me, and her distress was now acute. 'What is it about these ... these pearls there is all this fuss?' she asked, her English cracking at the strain of her predicament. It happened when she was excited, and then her tenses were apt to go awry too.

'They are special ones.'

'Yes, they are very nice, *très jolies, bien sûr*, but...'

To you, my darling, they are just shiny beads, *hein*?

'You see, they were given to Sybil by King Zog.'

'Sog?'

'No, Zog. Zzz....'

'He was King of England?'

'Albania.'

'*Vraiment* ... I see.'

Albania, Ruritania, it was all the same to Céline. It hardly mattered. Tuesday follows Monday, and so on *ad infinitum*. And where was Moses when the light went out? Facts are facts; they are of no deep concern. Céline knew things I didn't know, many things, the wisdom of ancient China sang in her bones.

I, too, had prevaricated enough about the bloody pearls. I decided to act. It was high time I made my position clear in relation to Céline. I would go with her to the police station, but there was something important I wanted to do first. I had passed on Arabella's jewellery to Daphne, save for two pieces. One was her wedding-ring, which I myself now wore, while the other was a solitaire diamond ring that had once belonged to my mother, given to her on my birth by my father. Like my mother, Arabella had worn it on her little finger. I took it out of its box and put it on

Céline's next finger. It fitted her perfectly and seemed to sparkle anew with a fresh beauty against her silken skin in the afternoon light, as if itself reborn. Céline was so moved she couldn't bring herself to say anything but she reached up to my face and kissed me. I held her close for a moment, from compassion and to reassure her.

Policemen are simple-minded, they are favourably disposed towards the clean-cut look, the old school tie, short back and sides, that sort of thing. So before we set off I thought I'd better spruce myself up. I changed into a pair of smart grey flannel trousers and put on a clean cream poplin shirt with an Italian silk tie, over which I wore a dark-blue linen jacket. I tilted my panama hat jauntily and then, a final touch, put a red silk handkerchief in my breast pocket in front of the looking-glass. 'The Great Gatsby,' I said in an undertone. Then: 'Do I pass muster?'

'Mustard? You are a funny man,' Céline said uncomprehending, though peering up at me admiringly.

'Sometimes,' I said. I touched the brim of my hat and gave her a small bow. 'I am at your service, *madame*. Come, let's go.'

It's a funny language.

I accompanied her in the police car, and then at the police station I explained that Céline was my fiancée, we were to be married shortly, almost implying within the hour, and that I hoped therefore they wouldn't want to detain her for long. Céline was quick to take my signal and put her hand on my arm, flashing her diamond ring as she did so. We called each other 'darling' quite a lot in a short space of time, rather putting it on. The investigating detective sergeant, a polite man, had instantly recognised me from his visit to Saxton House so that there was no need for me to produce my credentials. Rosie must have already satisfied him that my character, along with that of her other patients, was unimpeachable.

174

It amused me, I must say, to play the Upright Citizen. What a touch of soap and a decent tie can do for a man! Values never really seemed to change, to progress, I thought.

It was all over quite quickly. No, said the sergeant, there was nothing of any new significance they wanted to ask Miss Chen, it was just the continuation of a 'routine enquiry'. Yet he went over the same ground, asked Céline the same questions – when had she last seen the pearl necklace, at what time approximately had she last seen Lady Ayres-Southey, etcetera, etcetera. If the police still suspected her, it must have been partly because she was a foreigner, I imagined, but clearly they had nothing positive to go on, nothing they could justifiably pin on her. And maybe they were reluctant to cross swords with so evident a paragon of virtue as her fiancé.

I think my hat, which I held in my hand like a bridal bouquet at the police station, may well have helped clinch things, and that dash of Bolshevik red in my breast pocket.

14

We announced our engagement at the nursing home that same day. There was a rustle of surprise, though the other nurses must have already cottoned on. Rosie, perhaps to mask her disappointment, was quite effusive, throwing her arms around me and kissing me on both cheeks. It had been a near miss for us, I thought, but for practical reasons it could never have worked out if we had come together. I shouldn't have wanted to stay chained to Saxton House, taking on Denbigh's role, hanging about the village until one day I might eventually have to re-enter the home as one of Rosie's patients. The idea of being recycled in such a way was too droll, too ironic to contemplate. Céline gave a month's notice, and the week before we left Rosie arranged a small farewell party for us, at which Ingrid played some of my favourite Schubert and we were presented with two handsome travelling cases as a wedding present. Time, which in the past had often dragged with a dread monotony, accelerated towards the end, faces and images seeming to rush by in spasms like those glimpsed from a speeding train, which is why I find it difficult to recapture them.

Of course I had a pang, leaving my friends behind. They had been not so much like an extended family to me as travelling companions on a catalytic voyage to some dreamed-of planet, fellow-passengers who became infirm and enfeebled by their passage in the cramped and confining spaceship that took us circling past the outer galaxies, and who, when at last we touched down at our final destination, unaware of the glittering terrain I was fortunate to perceive from my angle of vision, peered blankly out of the familiar fly-bespattered windows, then turned to each other and exclaimed, 'Oh look, nothing has changed, it's just as it was at the beginning, it's the same place we thought we had left behind', and then continued munching their daily bread. Most of all I would miss Trudi, dear, good, emancipated Trudi, beside whom I had sat in our dizzy interplanetary circuit and upon whose willing shoulder I had heaped some of the burden of my frustrations those times I had awoken not as a weightless traveller in space but like a wanderer in grief from my blue garden.

When endings are transmuted into beginnings, new adventures come apace. Within seconds that pleasant dream in which you were drifting, floating along as in a still sea, can be uptilted and you find yourself clawing at the edge of a nightmare. We were in our cabin in the Channel ferry when it happened. I might have guessed that nothing would run smoothly for long. Perhaps it won't seem like much when I set it down, in certain respects there is an all too familiar ring to it, but in a sense it changed everything, so that nothing was quite the same ever again.

A happy ending? Judge for yourself if you will.

It was early afternoon, I remember, when Céline decided to have a shower. It had been hot on deck and the boat's lounges and resting areas were too congested with tourists for comfort. She seemed to take ages, but I wasn't in the least concerned; she wasn't likely to drown. I was lying reading on my bunk when at last she reappeared.

She was stark naked. For a moment she stood in a statuesque pose, with her right arm bent, her hand half across her breasts, her left arm curling down towards her crotch. She had let her hair down so that it fell sweeping along her left arm. In fact her pose had an almost uncanny resemblance to that of the flowing figure standing in a shell in *The Birth of Venus*, which made me wonder if it had been this quality in Céline that had hooked André like a goggle-eyed swimmer prowling in the *eau-de-Nil* shallows of a Renaissance ocean. However, there was one particular, one vital detail, by which Céline's nakedness was transformed. Instead of the coils of red hair hanging from around the shoulders of Venus as in Botticelli's masterpiece, there was suspended a magnificent necklace of pearls. Black pearls. They reached well below Céline's dried pip of a navel and almost to between her legs. She tilted her head to the right, again like Venus, and then gave me a coy smile, which was her very own.

Outrage quickly displaced my dismay and astonishment. I shouted at Céline, I don't know what precisely, and then I leaped from my bunk and tore the pearls from her neck with such force that it swung sideways as if her head might snap off. In doing so I broke the necklace, sending clusters of pearls spinning across the floor of the cabin. I picked up some of them, I didn't quite know what I was doing I was in such a state of shock. I felt betrayed. I'd throw them overboard, anything, to get rid of them somehow. But then I thought, in a cool instant of sanity, I always seemed to be throwing valuable jewellery away. It was a dire compulsion. Then an awful, wrecking question surged into my head: with Céline's palpable lies, her fantasies, her half-truths, what in God's name was I letting myself in for?

'I am sick of your lies,' I cried out despairingly. 'You never stop lying!'

Her hands went to her ravaged neck as her eyes filled with tears.

'*Tu te trompes!* It is not fair what you say, Michel. *Non, non, non! Ce n'est pas vrai!* Sybil, she give me the pearls. She tell me, I want you to have them, Jackie. You keep them for yourself, you hide them away and tell no one. *No one.* She was all right up here' – Céline pointed to her head – 'when she tell me. She say her niece ... Ethel? – very well, Elspeth – would snoop ... *non*, swoop down, but she say she don't like her. She don't want her to have them, to lay her sticky hands on the pearls....'

Her eyes, like her tenses, were wild.

'Caspar...?' I tried.

'Caspar – Sybil say he *hated* the pearls. You see, Sybil says ... she said he was jealous. He was jealous of King ... King Sog.'

'Zog.'

'Sog.'

'No, Zog, for God's sake, Céline. Zzz.'

'*Zzzog....* Anyhow, that's what Sybil tell me.'

I said nothing. I couldn't think of anything to say.

'It is *true.* Sybil give me ... gave me the pearls. Why don't you believe me, *chéri?* You *never* believe what I tell you.... Oh, I *love* you, don't you see? I don't lie to you because I *love* you – cross my heart, like you say.'

Then in a frantic but loving gesture she pummelled my chest with her fists.

Caspar disliked the pearls – that was true.

Céline loved me. That also I knew was true. Or I thought I knew.

Two out of two. A good beginning after all. A new leaf?

'Why can't you *leave* and let *leave?* Why can't you believe me when I tell you the truth? You make me so ... so *bouleversée*, so angry.'

'Live and let live' was one of my tiresome pet phrases and, rightly, Céline was telling me to eat my own words, choke on them. There was authenticity in what she

179

insisted Sybil had said to her – about Elspeth swooping down on the pearls and wanting to lay her sticky hands on them. These were Sybil's words, very much what she would have said in the circumstances. I could hear her saying them. And Caspar's so-called jealousy of King Zog – clearly that wasn't Céline's invention, it would have made little sense to her, the good King signified nothing to her.

But then, to put the clock back a stage further, what of the diamond bracelet? Should I simply wipe that off the slate, never mind that I'd been the one ultimately to get rid of it? The point was, I couldn't be sure of Céline's entanglement in that escapade, of how serious it was. I couldn't be sure of anything. What was remarkable, what had stuck in my mind as much as anything, as much as the actual theft, in which I too had had a hand through my very intervention between Céline and her pursuers, was her indifference to its disappearance, her total unconcern. That unconcern in itself suggested an intrinsic innocence. And her ingenuousness, that innocence of hers, I recognised, was profound. Its essence was primitive. It seemed to me when I unleashed the vision of my mind that in her rhythm of life she slipped like a fish with the currents; that she read the wind like a bird; that like a sylvan creature she ran when threatened for the cover of trees. So what was it about the drowned bracelet that mattered so much that I should wish to dispossess this child of the elements? What did it matter about the pearls? What did any of it matter?

And then I knew. I knew, not from any searing revelation, but through the quiet insistence of my senses. I knew deep within myself, as I must have known all along yet failed out of my innate fear of the future to translate into acceptance, that come what may I could never let her go.

'I believe you,' I cried. 'I believe you!'

I meant that I believed unequivocally in all I could perceive of her.

She looked so happy, so purified when I came out with these simple words of contrition, it helped discharge my mixed and contradictory feelings towards her, my feelings of shame and guilt from rejecting her pained entreaties, from refusing to heed them, and from the ugly prejudices to which I became prone when I tamely imbibed the bromide of convention, which etherised my understanding like a dulled nerve.

I held her hard and long in her mermaid nakedness as if after diving for her in the deep and then, saying nothing, like silent swimmers, we sank down together and started collecting the pearls, which lay scattered on the cabin floor like a precious harvest. And as we crouched there, sliding our hands back and forth like probing tentacles, I took Céline and kissed her and we began to make love amid the kingly treasure, Sybil's triumphal legacy. After a while she straddled me, gently rocking her silvery, lubricious body upon mine until I felt a stray pearl teasing my back, as if I lay in the oyster shell that had yielded it like the birth of a single shining star in a hidden drift of the universe. I retrieved it with one hand and held it between my forefinger and thumb close to her face. 'Be a good girl,' I said laughing and with all the joy of rediscovery, 'and I'll give you a pearl.'

She put her wet lips round it and took the pearl in her mouth. For a moment I thought she might swallow it as she swirled it around her gums. Then, raising her eyes heavenwards as if invoking her celestial kin and puffing up her cheeks like a cherub, she blew the pearl playfully back at me.

LATER

All life is a dream, and dreams are dreams.

Pedro Calderón de la Barca

Arabella and I found this place, stumbling on it by luck after a long drive through France on one of our expeditions to the South. We felt so drawn to it we toyed with the idea of coming to live here ourselves. I suppose it can be unwise if not dangerous to retrace steps one has taken with someone else, especially when emotions are involved, and I have made no secret of this past link of mine. However, Céline doesn't seem to mind at all. She left it entirely to me to decide where we should settle, and frankly I had neither the inclination nor the energy to cruise to and fro looking for some virgin location, virgin in the sense of somewhere neither of us had set foot in before. Besides, although I only half admit it to myself, I think my globe-trotting days are pretty well over. At last the grass is greener where I happen to be.

We live in a charming, airy apartment with stone-flagged floors and a wide balcony looking on to the market square in the old part of the town, which has that special intimate community atmosphere of a village, and it hasn't taken long for us to be accepted, invited into the fold, by the local people, though maybe to begin with they thought we made a somewhat incongruous couple. Apart from the offerings of the weekly market, in which because of its proximity we can almost participate without venturing outdoors, there is a delightful mix of food shops and others, and at the small restaurants and cafés dotted about you can sit outside for most months of the year to pass the time of day.

The town has ancient origins, reaching back to the Roman settlement, evidence of which can be seen in ruins of an amphitheatre and a forum, constructed of a greenish local stone apparently much favoured at the time and still used, as well as a bath complex, while here and there you can see pieces of Roman mosaic with strange, esoteric motifs of mythic beasts which seize the imagination. The cathedral adjoining the market-place, the dong of whose bells reverberates in our home as down the ages it must have boomed over the half-timbered houses, is of the tenth century, and one of our pleasures is to attend the regular concerts held in this cool haven by local as well as visiting musicians. Napoleon Bonaparte prayed here, when he stopped off in the town on his march north after his escape from Elba to rally his armies before the Hundred Days. Yet although the house where he lodged at the edge of the town is commemorated with a plaque, it has become neglected, being inhabited these days mostly by pigeons and mice, and where his aides once scurried back and forth at his mesmeric behest, rats scuttle along the cobwebbed passages.

It is not a spectacular or fashionable place to live, which is one of its charms, and else the world and his wife would descend as they do in the summer months along so much of the Côte d'Azur. Even so, tourists do obtrude on the sandy beach, which I tend to avoid altogether, though Céline traipses there for a swim in the sea, her lustred limbs soaped by bubbling spume as she dives through the waves. In her white smock and with her plaited hair she looks quaintly oriental as she wanders down the long, wide avenue of tropical trees that leads to the shore, like a figure on a plate. She has ceased doing so latterly, since, much to her delight, she is bearing our child. I'm a bit long in the tooth for fatherhood, I dare say, but Pip, who I thought might be querulous about it or even resentful, seems genuinely intrigued by the prospect of having so young a sibling. He says he wants us to bring our baby to visit him and his brood in America next year.

Céline's pregnancy has had a calming influence on both of us, which we needed badly after those last traumatic weeks in England, and we are leading a restorative, contented life. Céline loves to sit making her baby clothes on our balcony, from which she can wave, fluttering a butterfly hand, at her new friends passing by. Her Hollywood star-spotting is in full spate too. For instance the dapper proprietor of the café beneath our first-floor apartment, his Gallic moustache as distinctive as the blue-and-white striped awning of his premises, is another Adolphe Menjou, and the present mayor of the town with his bulbous nose is the living image of Schnozzle Durante. As for women, the stars among them – mostly the visitors – are legion, and one day I had a quite pointless squabble with Céline about the eyes – or was it eyelashes? – of Loretta Young and Norma Shearer, reminiscent of the silly arguments I used to have with Arabella about directions. Occasionally when we drive to Cannes for the day Céline sees a real, contemporary film star on the wing, but for her these *arriviste* performers have nothing on the old glories studding her celluloid firmament.

I've been kept busy completing this much-thumbed account of my days at Saxton House, taking care not to revise what I wrote earlier on, especially about Céline, with the benefit of hindsight. Life is in a continual flow and nothing remains constant, and so it is with one's experiences, viewed inexorably from different points of time. Even my blue garden has moved away, and those days and nights when I anticipated escaping beyond its opaque barrier have themselves receded as into a dream within a dream. Yet if I lack the will or desire to re-explore the endless streets and avenues along which I was persuaded in my quest for Arabella, seeking an explanation for her death, if I can no longer bring myself to re-examine the shimmering images they evoked frame by frame, fixed in my heart and mind as a symbol of recovery my blue garden will continue illumining the inner dark.

As for Arabella, never a day goes by when I do not think of her, and at night she wells up in my sleep on a tide of memories, so vividly at times that when I awake I reach out, imagining I can touch her dear body, curled up in a bundle like an infant in a womb, her arms hugging her shoulders in that particular, protective way of hers. But of course it is Céline whom I find lying beside me, and when she accepts the caress of my fingers as intended for herself she responds with a sweet sigh and holds my hand against her cool cheek. At once my feeling that I have been deceiving her with my amaranthine love for another is overtaken by one of renewed contentment at rediscovering her by my side and I think, Oh lucky man.

So, will my luck be lasting? Come break of day and its sobering draughts of early light, I sometimes switch back stealthily, almost unconsciously, to a commonplace but needed awareness of the stark reality of what I then conceive as my aleatoric situation; into a state of detachment anyway from my all too gullible romanticism. Then I say to myself, I shall endeavour to hold on to Céline as best I can for as long as I can. Though simply because of my age quite as much as her very unpredictability, of which I have already endured painful stabs in the past, my days with her must surely be numbered. And it is during these intermittent moments of – shall I say, lucidity, or plain cynicism? – that I tell myself that I rushed her into marriage on a compulsive wave of passion, possessiveness certainly; and, moreover, that all along I have been bewitched by a sneak-thief, a sly opportunist, who is just as likely to discard me, and every bit as summarily, as she divested herself of the diamond bracelet on that fateful day in the Jardin du Luxembourg. Of course I muffle these jagged thoughts sagely under my pillow the rest of the while, willing them not to spike our gossamer Eden.

The question of veracity or proof of ownership aside, we haven't had the pearls restrung. Céline doesn't want to wear them. Instead she has placed them loose in a cardboard box at her bedside, just as Sybil had them. She is keeping them, so she says, as a nest-egg or nest-eggs for our child. Quite a nest-egg. Quite as lustrous – illustrious – as, say, some imperial ovoid laid by Fabergé. Yet I doubt if a casual intruder would pay this drab little casket any attention, probably mistaking its contents for a clutch of worthless trinkets. Céline takes them out of the box sometimes and cradles them, entranced, in her cupped hands as though she has scooped the black marvels, sea-wet and irradiant, from some secret marine cavity. One can find solace in a sense of possession.